"Earth exists," said Zalman. "Or, at least, I know of a man who swears it does. I will take you to him and from him you may learn what it is you wish to know. My share of our agreement. Yours?"

"I have nothing you can use," Dumarest answered.

"So you say but I am convinced otherwise. Well, it can wait. I trust you. Later, after you have met the man I spoke of we will talk again." Zalman rose, stretching, "Shall we go?"

"To where?"

"The field. To find a ship and book passage. The man you want is on Elysius."

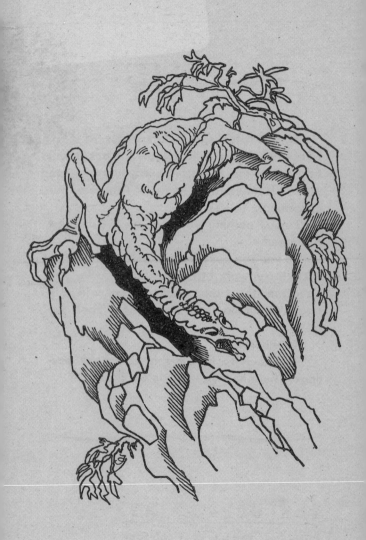

THE
TERRA
DATA

E. C. Tubb

DAW BOOKS, INC.

DONALD A. WOLLHEIM, PUBLISHER
1633 Broadway
New York, N.Y.   10019

To: CLAIRE LOUISE ELCOMB

FIRST PRINTING, APRIL 1980

1 2 3 4 5 6 7 8 9

DAW TRADEMARK REGISTERED
U.S PAT. OFF. MARCA REGISTRADA.
HECHO EN U.S.A.

PRINTED IN U.S.A.

Chapter ONE

————◆◆◆◆————

In the dark a child was crying.

Listening to it, a normal man would have responded to the thin, keening wail, feeling the emptiness, the terror and hopeless despair, but to Elge it was merely the symptom of a disturbing problem. The thing crying had been old long before he'd been born, and tears, to it, had been alien for the major part of its life. Yet now it cried as if a child again. Why?

"Catatonia," said the man at his side. Like Elge he wore the scarlet robe of the Cyclan. His face was gaunt, bone prominent, his skull devoid of hair; attributes common to all cybers. "The probability is so high as to eliminate doubt. For some reason the intelligence is trying to find escape in the past."

Moving back through time into childhood—there to find forgotten terrors. An answer which was almost certainly correct; Icelus was too skilled to make errors, but one which left the main problem unsolved. Why should the intelligence have needed to escape at all?

Leaning back in his chair Elge stared thoughtfully at the console before him; the meters, readouts, signal lights, the speakers from which came the endless sobbing. Crude apparatus compared to what alternatives were available but far safer to use as two cybers had proved; one now dead from cerebral shock, the other a mindless shell. And yet a probability remained that he could gain some measure of success.

A touch and a microphone was activated. "Itel," said

Elge. "Itel, can you hear me? Answer if you can. Answer!"

The sobbing continued.

"Itel?" A waste of time and energy; the intelligence had reverted to before the name had been given. A fact Icelus would have known but he had remained silent, content to watch, to gauge the other's ability. Elge said, "You have his dossier?"

He waited as it was fed into a machine; a minute chip which held the sum total of a man's active existence. The details flashed on the screen were what he'd expected; a child of the slums spotted by a shrewd agent and placed in a Cyclan school for elementary training. Proving worthy he had become first an acolyte then, later, had won the scarlet robe of a cyber. A man trained and tested and dedicated to serving the organization; one as efficient as a living machine. Itel had served well in that he had never failed and had earned his final reward. A reward he had enjoyed for centuries—why should he now be crying?

"As I told you," said Icelus when Elge asked the question. "Catatonia."

"The condition but not the cause."

"True—that is, as yet, unknown." He added, as Elge remained silent, "All possible causes have been eliminated by a series of exhaustive tests. The nutrient fluids have been analyzed and found innocuous. No trace of radiation was found in the casing or attendant structures. No chemical alterations of any kind could be discerned in any part of the essential apparatus. There is no apparent protoplasmic degeneration."

"But there is a correlation with previous breakdowns." Elge studied the addendum on the dossier. "This unit was removed from its original position and placed in isolation."

"To minimize the risk of contamination," explained Icelus. "It was previously in close proximity to a bank of failed units."

Brains which had taken to uttering nothing but gibberish—the entire unit of which they were a part totally destroyed by orders of the Cyber Prime. A decision which, obviously, had failed to achieve the desired result. Elge listened again to the thin, frightened wailing of a lost and lonely child. What was it seeking? How did it feel? A brain, taken from its skull, fitted with life-support apparatus, placed in a vat of nutrient fluids there to rest, alive, awake and aware. Once it had been a part of Central Intelligence; incorporated in the massed brains which, linked together, formed the tremendous cybernetic computer able to handle an incredible input of data. Able also to eliminate time and space in direct communication with cybers scattered throughout the galaxy. The heart of the Cyclan—one now at risk.

Elge recognized the danger as did others. A unit could fail and, if that failure was due to a malfunction of apparatus, it could be accepted. But if a unit should fail for no apparent reason then to punish the attendants was not enough. The cause had to be found and eliminated. *Had* to! The merest acolyte could predict the disaster implicit in the disintegration of the Central Intelligence. At all costs that disaster must be avoided.

The screen died as Elge touched a control; data vanishing as the chip was automatically expelled. Facts he had assimilated and could always check if the need arose but which now served no useful purpose. The sound of weeping followed, to be replaced by a sudden, almost tangible silence. One broken by a rustle as Icelus moved.

"The Council will be expecting your attendance," he said. "They may wish to hear your conclusions."

"There is time." Minutes and to a cyber a minute was not to be wasted, yet what more could he do? Elge rose, conscious of a sudden chill, wondering at its origin. The body was a machine and not to be cosseted for fear of it becoming less efficient. Food was fuel and fat excess tissue, hampering, unwanted, yet at times the loss of insulation made itself felt. He must increase his diet a little, there was an optimum balance to be maintained; in the meantime a walk would restore his efficiency. One through the caverns of the headquarters of the Cyclan.

An earlier age would have called it a temple; a place

built to house a subterranean god, formed, adorned, tended by devoted priests. But no earlier age could have imagined the vastness of the huge complex which lay in calculated array miles beneath the surface of a scarred and lonely world. Yet the similarity remained; the mathematical form of the caverns designed for maximum strength held the beauty of functional design, the cybers were dedicated servants and if a god was something more than a man the Central Intelligence was all of that. And, like a god, it had its sacrifice.

Alone in his office Master Nequal, Cyber Prime, sat and contemplated the nearing conclusion of his life. It had been a long one; the stamp of years accentuated the skull-like appearance of his face which formed a waxen ball against the rich scarlet of his thrown-back cowl. An old face for it takes time to achieve great power and he had started as a starving boy begging in a gutter, stealing when the opportunity arose, fighting like an animal when, inevitably, he had been caught. Then the school, the strange men with their strange ways, the lessons instilled by pain, the promises and the proofs, the growing desire to be as they were; men indifferent to the normal world, protected from it, respected for the attributes they possessed.

The skilled talent he had nurtured and had brought to flower.

One which now had turned against him.

To know. To have the ability as every cyber had to extrapolate from a handful of known facts and to predict the logical sequence of events. To gauge and evaluate and to reach a conclusion that was so probable as to be almost certain. And he knew his inevitable fate.

He would die. A death earned because he had failed and even though he was the Cyber Prime still he had to pay the penalty of failure. To die. To be robbed of his hoped-for reward. Never to rest in blissful freedom of the irritations of the body and enjoy the pleasure of mental expansion. Of tasting the joy of mental achievement—the only pleasure a cyber could know.

An end he had anticipated all through the long, long years of his dedicated service.

A lamp glowed on the panel before him followed by a voice as he touched a stud. "Master?"

"Yes?"

"The Council is assembling." Jarvet, his aide, and one who said too little. Yandron would have said more but he was dead now, long gone to his reward, wondering, perhaps, why his old master was taking so long to join himself and the rest in mental gestalt. "Master?"

"I heard."

A pause as if of waiting then the lamp died as Jarvet broke the connection. Had he hoped for more? Unnecessary repetition? Questions of an empty nature? If so he had been disappointed. If almost a century of life failed to teach a man discretion then he had better never to have been born.

But the years rode heavily. Nequal straightened, slowly, using the desk to gain support until he was firmly upright. A thing which would have told against him had any been present to observe and they would have been right to condemn him. A cyber had to be efficient at all times and the Cyber Prime most of all. Why had he waited so long?

The answer bloomed before him as he activated a familiar control.

It was a masterpiece of electronic ingenuity; tiny motes of light held in a mesh of invisible forces, the entire galactic lens constrained within three hundred cubic feet of space. With such compression details had to be lost; the billions of individual worlds, the comets, the asteroidal matter, rogue planets, isolated patches of dust, all swallowed in the glowing depiction of countless stars. Nequal touched a control and scarlet flecks appeared in scattered profusion, each fleck representing a cyber. More than there had been when he first became Cyber Prime to rest at the very apex of his world, but not as many as he would have liked. Still there were large areas devoid of the scarlet flecks, spaces in which they were thinly scattered, regions and nodes in which the influence of the Cyclan was minor or absent. More evidence of his failure but none other than himself would have considered it as such. It was a personal assessment of how far he had failed to reach the goal he had set himself when the Council had elevated him to his present position. And yet, even when setting that target, he had known he would fail.

Ambition, even the emotionless aspirations of a cyber, had to accept the limitations of reality. It took time for a cyber to gain the trust of a ruler. More to make himself indispensable. Years and even decades before the domination of the Cyclan could be so firmly established that nothing could shake it. And the galaxy was so vast, the worlds so plentiful, the task so great that it seemed it would never be accomplished. That sheer size and distance would thwart the Great Plan and frustrate the ideal which governed his life and the lives of all who wore the scarlet robe. To dominate everyone everywhere. To eliminate waste. To establish the law of logic and reason wherever mankind could be found.

An aim to which he had dedicated his life.

One shortly to end.

"Master!" Jarvet had arrived in person, now standing within the open door, his eyes like his face as impassive as if carved from stone. "The Council—"

"Are waiting my presence. I understand."

"No, master. They are willing to excuse you if that is what you wish."

A deference to his rank while reinforcing the fact that they were the real strength of the Cyclan. A guard and check against dangerous excess or reluctant tardiness; watchdogs to keep the Cyber Prime at his best. He could sit and wait and their decision would be delivered but they, and he, knew what it would be. Or he could attend and face those who chose to accuse him and defend the actions he had taken. A choice which was really no choice at all.

"I shall not keep them waiting." The glowing depiction died to form splintered shards of fading luminescence. A brilliance against which the normal, bluish glow seemed dull by contrast. "Go ahead and inform the Council I am on my way."

They stirred as he entered the chamber, a dozen men who appeared as brothers, uniform in their robes, each blazoned with the great Seal of the Cyclan on the breast. Shaven heads bowed and fabric rustled as they resumed their seats. Nequal, when they had settled, walked to his own at the head of the table.

Before sitting he said, "I am aware of the purpose of this meeting and commend it. I have also given thought to the one who should succeed me as, I know, you have also. But, until he does, I remain the Cyber Prime. As such I am willing to be questioned."

Not ritual but a statement of intent; the Cyclan had no time for empty formalities. From a point down the table a man said, "Before we vote should we hear the summation of events?"

"Unnecessary." Dekel, his face as thin as a razor, did not look at the speaker. "I put the question direct; Master Nequal, do you agree that you have outlived your usefulness as Cyber Prime?"

"I do."

"Then we are agreed. A summation will serve no useful purpose."

"Yet there is no need of haste." Thern, older, his face a trifle rounder, added his comment. "And there is still a question to be decided."

"Have I merited the reward of success." Nequal knew what it had to be. "Who accuses me of failure?"

Boule was the first to speak. "I for one. You failed in your treatment of the degenerated brains as later events have demonstrated. And you have failed to regain the lost secret of the affinity twin."

Facts, but how could he have acted other than he had as regards the brains? Units had gone apparently insane and had to be divorced from the main assembly. To destroy them had seemed the wisest course. As for the other—he had no defense.

"Vote." The voice was emphatic. "The final decision may be left to the new Cyber Prime."

The new deciding how to dispose of the old and how he chose to do so would be noted. Nequal took the paper before him; it held three names and, without hesitation, he marked one with a bold tick. Others did the same and he was certain whom they had chosen. The same man as himself—a simple matter of logical extrapolation.

Rising he said, "With your permission I shall return to my office. After Cyber Elge has been informed of his new status perhaps he will come to claim it."

He entered softly, standing to look at the dimensions of the place, the severely functional lines. Only the glowing depiction gave life and color, painting Nequal's face with dancing motes, accentuating the hollows, the lines, the passage of years. It was time and more than time for him to be replaced and yet it was not easy for Elge to dismiss him. The man had worked too hard, had served too long for that. Not sentiment, but the appreciation of merit— and if nothing else he was owed that.

Without moving his eyes from the depiction Nequal said, "Your decision?"

"You failed."

"And so merit erasure. To be turned into basic elements, brain, body and bone." Extinction, his awareness terminated, complete and total disintegration. "The brains?"

"The degeneration has not been halted. From my study of the previous breakdown I find you at fault for ordering the destruction of the units in question. Saved, they could have yielded information of value. There is even the possibility they could have been progressing to a higher framework of mental reference using concepts which we failed to understand."

"And so, logically, I could have destroyed a higher intelligence." Nequal lifted his head, reflected light glowing from his eyes. "I refute the possibility. Even if it existed nothing was lost. The units were old and if the progression was an attribute of age then other units would have shown similar symptoms. If the decay was not of that nature then it was imperative to avoid contamination."

"Tests showed there was no danger of that."

"On a physical level, perhaps. I was thinking of a paraphysical contamination. An insane person can affect others and alter their appreciation of reality. The same could apply to the brains. It was a possibility I had to consider."

And had been right to do so. Elge remembered the crying, the sound of a child from darkness. What if it should spread?

Nequal, watching, said, "You appreciate the dilemma. It was essential to gain time and to safeguard Central Intelligence. Analysis of the affected units revealed nothing which could have been a physical cause. Yet the problem remained."

As did the theories but none provided a solution to the cause.

Elge said, "And now?"

"A new development. A unit which has returned to childhood. Catatonia. I would assume that the condition has been induced by the isolation of the unit. And yet that seems too facile. My own fears are that a progressive degeneration could be taking place on a subconscious level and that it requires only a stimulus to complete the transformation from sane to aberrated response. If I am correct then all observed symptoms are relatively unimportant in that they are only various manifestations of the same disease."

Tears, gibberish, screams, babbling—how long before the Central Intelligence began to transmit false information?

"I have a suggestion." Nequal looked again at the glowing lens. "It could help to achieve direct communication with the catatonic unit. Electronic apparatus is too crude and the normal use of the Samatchazi formulae with the arousing of the grafted Homochon elements has proved too dangerous. However, should I be processed and linked to the affected unit, it is possible that I may be able to solve the entire problem."

A gamble and one he couldn't lose. Nequal was offer-

ing himself as a sacrifice in the hope of gaining near im-
mortality. If he succeeded he would be linked to the
massed brains—the reward he still hoped to achieve. If he
failed he would have lost nothing of value.

Elge said, "And the rest?"

"The affinity twin." Nequal's eyes moved from star to
star of the depiction. It changed as he manipulated a control, expanding, the edges thinning, vanishing as a part
gained greater detail. A smear of opaque dust in which
suns burned like angry coals. "The Rift," he said. "The
Quillian Sector. Harge."

"Dumarest?"

"Earl Dumarest, my real failure. The decaying units—
who can foretell what is to come with absolute certainty?
Always remains the unknown factor, the random, unpredictable element. A man named Brasque, for example,
who stole the secret from our laboratory on Riano. Who
gave it to his dying wife who used it to become young and
lovely. Who died in turn and who passed it on to
Dumarest. A wanderer. A traveler. A drifter among
worlds."

A man who had defeated the Cyclan and who'd merited death for the cybers he had killed. Who had, incredibly, managed to elude the traps set for him, the snares
designed to hold him fast.

Luck or something more? An attribute as unusual as
his physical prowess; the speed which had saved him so
often? Things which had failed him at the end.

"Fifteen molecular units," said Nequal as if speaking to
himself. "The reversal of one determining whether or not
it is subjective or dominant. We know the nature of the
units. We know that the chains enable a mind to take
over the being of another creature. To become that creature, animal or human, in almost total assimilation. All
we lack is the knowledge of the correct sequence in which
the units must be joined."

Fifteen units, the possible combinations were vast and
to try them all would take millennia even if one unit could
be fashioned and tested each second. An impossibility;

each unit took a minimum of eight hours to construct and test. A planet could grow old and turn into dust before all could be tried.

"We know he was in the Rift," said Nequal. "In the Quillian Sector. On Harge." His face thinned at the memory of it, the cyber who had paid for his stupidity. As he was about to pay for his failure in turn. His failure—always the Cyber Prime had to accept the final responsibility.

As Elge would do.

Nequal glanced at the man where he stood close to the depicted galaxy. He was relatively young and should live long; a factor which had governed his choice as it had the others for the Cyclan had no use for the old and ailing. Time would expand his horizons and he would build on the accomplishments of his predecessors. When his turn came to be replaced the simulacrum could be blazing with scarlet where now there was none. And he too could share in the achievement. As a living brain linked to Central Intelligence he would have helped to bring it about. But first Elge must make his decision.

He turned as if sensing Nequal's tension, speaking as if he had read the other's thoughts.

"Your offer," he said. "You accept that failure will result in extinction?"

"I do." There was no need to emphasize the converse—to destroy a successful unit would be illogical and inefficient and so alien to the workings of the Cyclan. Nequal added, "I am probably the most suitable instrument at your disposal."

A fact which Elge had already assessed as he had evaluated the survival-drive inherent in the older man. A factor which would augment the chance of his success and one not to be wasted.

Elge said, "Your offer is accepted. When will you be ready?"

"Immediately."

There was no point in delay. As the new Cyber Prime moved toward the desk and the communicator Nequal looked for the last time at the glowing depiction. A plethora of habitable worlds among which a lone man had moved. One who had bested him and the power at his command. Dumarest—had he really died?

Chapter TWO

At first the girl seemed grotesque; impossibly deformed as if stretched by some monstrous machine, then Dumarest realized the impression was one created by illusion and artifice. The pants which hugged the long, lithe legs were cut high at the waist and fell over stilted sandals to give an illusion of height. One aided by the tightly cinctured waist, the narrow shoulders lifted by tapered pads; the shortening of the neck masked by a cascade of purple hair which rose in an elaborate bouffant to tower high above the rounded skull.

"Dumarest? Earl Dumarest?" The mirrored lenses covering her eyes gave her the expressionless stare of an insect. "Is that your name?"

"Why do you ask?"

"Because if it is I've a message for you." She stepped closer and his nostrils filled with the scent of her perfume; a rich, floral odor which hung about her like a cloud. "Aren't you going to ask me in?"

The room was small, one of the cheapest the hotel provided, the furnishings to match: a narrow bed, a chair, a cabinet, a small table on which stood a vase filled with delicate blooms. Their scent warred with the girl's.

"No wine?" She looked at the chair then sat on the bed. "I was told you were generous."

"By whom?"

"A mutual friend." She leaned back, resting her weight on her arms, inflating her chest so as to display the high prominence of her breasts. "You could send for some

wine and then we could have a nice, friendly drink.
Wouldn't you like that?"

Dumarest said, flatly, "Get out!"

"Why, don't you like me?" Her smile was a mechanical
invitation. "I'm not so hard to get along with. My guess is
that you're lonely, right? A stranger and short of company. Why make it so hard? Just send for some wine and
we can relax and talk and be friendly. Real friendly, mister, you'd like that." She smiled again as his hand lifted
and moved slowly toward her cheek. "You want to touch
me, honey? Feel how warm I am? Remember how—"
She broke off, snarling. "Bastard!"

She dressed as a girl and spoke as one and acted as one
but her naked eyes betrayed her. Dumarest looked at
them, the mirrored lenses hanging from the fingers of his
left hand. Old, hard, resembling splintered glass fogged
and brittle with time. Eyes which had seen too much and
had given up trying. His own noted the tiny lines at their
corners, the deeper lines buried beneath the paint, the
telltale signs of cosmetic surgery undergone more than
once. A harpy plying her trade in hotels, latching on to
the lonely, the strangers willing to accept her company.

What would she have slipped into his wine?

"Out!" He threw the lenses into her lap. "Get out!"

"And if I don't?"

She could have an in with the manager who would
come at her scream to back her accusation of rape. A
farce—but who would care about a stranger? Staring at
her Dumarest saw her face change, the eyes grow wide
with fear, the lips thinning as she hunched back on the
bed.

"No! Mister, for God's sake!"

He looked down at his hand, at the knife clenched in it,
drawn from his boot in instinctive response to danger.
Light shone from the blade, clouding on the wickedly
curved edges, the needle point. Light which vanished as
he thrust it back into its sheath.

"You wanted to kill me," she whispered. "You would
have killed me if—God! What kind of man are you?"

Not the kind she thought but he made no effort to

change her opinion. Let her think he would have killed her if it would mean an avoidance of trouble. Such a reputation could save him from others with similar intentions.

"Out," he said. "I won't tell you again."

She writhed on the bed, passing him, her perfume now contaminated by another scent; the raw reek of fear. At the door she paused, turning to face him, her eyes again shielded behind mirror lenses.

"What about your friend?"

"Don't you ever give up?"

"I mean it. How do you think I knew your name? How to find you?" She gave him no chance to answer. "He told me. All right, so I tried to make some extra profit, can you blame me for that? It's a hard life, mister, damned hard."

The more so when you were old and unwanted and trying to stay alive by selling goods which had long lost their appeal. Doing it and hating it and the necessity which gave you no choice. How often had he been in a similar situation? Driven to fight from pressing need? To risk his life in an arena, standing beneath glaring lights, ringed by avid faces, wounding, cutting, killing for the sake of continued survival.

"Mister?" Her tone held a note of pleading and despite the illusive height she seemed somehow small and helpless. "Earl—please. I get nothing if you don't show."

And how much for leading him into a trap? She could be innocent but what else could it be? He knew no one in this world so who could have sent for him but those he had reason to know meant him harm?

"Earl?"

"Just be on your way."

"I did it all wrong," she said regretfully. "Now you don't trust me. Well, I guess I can't blame you for that. But at least let me take back a message. Shall I ask your friend to call? Would that be more convenient for you?"

Age had dulled her intelligence—if the one who'd sent her wanted or had been willing to call why use an intermediary? Her visit could have been simply to locate him;

now he would have to move and forfeit the advance paid on the room. An expense he could have done without. Funds were low and he had still to find a passage. To delay too long could be fatal.

"Well?" The woman was still waiting. "Shall I tell him to call?"

"Yes." The harm was done and it would send her on her way. "Tell him I'll expect him tonight. An hour after sunset. And remind him to bring some wine." He added, casually, without change of tone, "What was his name again?"

"Bochner, didn't I tell you? Leo Bochner."

The woman had lied; the man was not the hunter. Bochner had been tall, slim, his face unlined, his hands smooth as was his voice. The camouflage of the animal resting beneath his skin. The man he now faced could also be an animal, a man dedicated to the love of destruction, one who lusted after the spilling of blood, but if so it was buried deep. He came forward, smiling, one hand extended in an ancient gesture of friendship.

"Earl! It was good of you to come." Their fingers touched, parted. "Zalman," he said. "Hans Zalman. What did you think of my messenger?"

"The best you could get?"

"The most suitable. No, she won't talk. The money I gave her will be spent on drugs and she will spend days in hallucinogenic diversions. My errand will become a part of them. Some wine?"

He poured without waiting for an answer, his hands deft as they manipulated bottle and glasses. A man a head shorter than Dumarest, rounder, his face creased with soft living. His clothing was expensive; pants and blouse of harmonizing color, his boots softly supple, the belt adorned with arabesques of precious metal. A man of apparent wealth and occupying a room which could not have been cheap.

"I have money," he said. "Not as much as I would like but enough for immediate needs. No, I do not intend to drug you or cause you any harm of any kind. We are alone in this apartment, search it if you wish. I am not expecting visitors. Bochner is not here."

Answers to questions Dumarest hadn't asked but had formed in his mind. Zalman gave another.

"Bochner is dead."

"How?"

"His stupidity killed him. He made the mistake of underestimating those who wear a scarlet robe."

The Cyclan—what did this man know of the organization?

"Enough to treat them as you would a venomous serpent. Which is to say," he added, "with wary respect. But your attitude would be different. In you, I think, respect would be absent."

Was the man a telepath?

"No." Zalman beamed as he sipped his wine. "I am not reading your mind but I am reading you all the same. The way you stand, move, the movement of the muscles of your face, the flick of your eyes, the tensions you emit—a hundred things. A talent I have had since early childhood. The ability to tell what a person is thinking from the tiny signals I glean from his body. You understand why I sent for you in the way I did, of course."

"To throw me off guard," said Dumarest. "What were you hoping to learn?"

"Your true identity. I was almost certain but there was the possibility of a mistake. Now I have no doubt. Some more wine?"

Dumarest had barely touched what he had. As Zalman refilled his own goblet he moved about the room studying the ornate decorations. Any of the protuberances could hold an electronic eye or ear. Already it could be too late.

"No!" Zalman was emphatic. "I give you my word this is not a trap."

How could it be trusted?

"A difficulty, I admit, but I swear it is so. I need to talk to you, Earl, to discuss a certain matter of mutual advantage. How to convince you I am exactly what I appear to be. Bochner? You want to know about Leo Bochner?"

Dumarest said, quickly, "Yes, but not here."

"You don't trust this place. A commendable caution. Where then? Your room? No." Zalman smiled. "Ideal! I have much to learn from you, my friend. The baths, but which? Earl, the choice is yours."

The city held many; palaces designed to cater to the wealthy, others merely providing a room full of steam for workers to ease their tensions. Between the two extremes could be found a host of variations. Dumarest chose one at random, staying close to Zalman as they changed, stepping into a marbled space filled with areas of colored smoke; steam which carried perfumes, stinging oils, stimulating drugs, changing novelties all confined by electronic barriers to selected regions.

In a cloud of emerald mist Dumarest learned how Bochner had died.

"As I said, he was a fool." Zalman, vague in the steam, peered at his companion. "You were together in the Quillian Sector and must have learned that. A man bemused by the mystique of killing. He thought of a hunt as a religious ritual and the actual killing as something more emotional than a sexual climax. For him it could have been the truth."

"You knew him well?"

"We met and, yes, I knew him. I knew when he lied and when he boasted and I knew the things he wanted to keep hidden. Some things I knew better then he did himself. He hated you as you must have guessed, but do you know why? It was because you spared him. You bested him in combat and had your blade to his throat and he stared into the face of the extinction he secretly craved and you spared him. When I met him he lived only to avenge the insult."

Dumarest could believe it. Leaning back he saw again the thin, contorted face, the naked savagery burning in the eyes. It would have been more merciful to have driven home the blade.

"Merciful, perhaps," said Zalman. "But had you not spared him we would not be sitting here now. As it was I met him barely in time. Luck, who can define it? A vessel which left sooner than I thought, a few days waiting and a chance meeting and then a voyage together in the same ship. Coincidence—but it happens. Sometimes more than we realize. Our meeting, for example. I saw you down at the field and knew you at once from Bochner's description. It was not too hard to follow you, to learn where you lived." His shrug stirred the scented vapor. "The rest you know."

"And Bochner?"

"Dead. His head shattered by some explosion. I was on a trip and learned of it when I returned."

The punishment meted out by the Cyclan for failure and Zalman's trip had probably saved his life. But what had he learned from the hunter?

"Something he barely suspected," he said. "Yet I know he had an inkling of what it must be. Something of incredible value to our friends of the scarlet robe which they would pay highly to obtain. Bochner was their agent, of course, and you must have suspected it. He was to trap you, hold you fast, but something happened to upset the plan." His hand waved in a gesture of negation. "That is of no importance now, the past is dead. But your importance remains and, I think, you are fully aware of your danger."

"So?"

"Something you have which the Cyclan wants," said Zalman. "Something of tremendous value to them at least. And, if it is valuable to them, why not to others? You see my point, Earl? I am suggesting that we share it and find the highest bidder. As I told you, a scheme to our mutual advantage."

One Dumarest wished he had never heard. Zalman, little as he knew of the man, had induced a liking and it made it harder to do what had to be done. In the emerald mist Dumarest lifted his hands, the fingers clamped fast to turn them into blunted axes, broad-bladed spears. A blow to the larynx would render the man helpless, doubled and retching, the nape of his neck exposed to a killing chop. Injuries which could be explained by an accidental fall on the moist tiles.

Murder—but how else to save himself?

Zalman had moved away and Dumarest looked for him, feeling the sting of unfamiliar odors in his nostrils, a sudden singing in his ears. The man had to die. Greed would make him dangerous and, even if he had no hint of the secret Dumarest carried locked in his mind, the insistance that he had a secret at all was enough.

"Earl?" Zalman's bulk showed wreathed in emerald. "What do you say?"

He was smooth, glistening, but the tissue covering his bones was muscle, not fat. The lowered chin made a slash at the throat difficult and the nape would be better protected than he had thought. The carotids, then, the great arteries leading to the brain. A pressure of his fingers would close them, bringing swift unconsciousness and eventual death. A more explicable termination than the other; the cause would be attributed to a cardiac failure.

"A partnership. We work together for—" Zalman glanced at the arm Dumarest had placed against his chest, the fingers which were now closing on his throat. He said, quietly, "Why?"

"I don't care for your idea of mutual advantage. I give you everything and you give me—what?" He was talking, delaying the moment. "I'm sorry, Hans."

"No!" Extra sweat beaded Zalman's face. "Give me a chance to explain. Earl!" He swallowed as the fingers eased a little. "For God's sake, man, listen. Your share I've mentioned now let me tell you of my contribution. I can guide you to Earth!"

Lies! Lies! It had to be lies!

"Earth!" Zalman pulled at the hand, the clamping fingers. "Earth, Earl! I know how to find it!"

The barrier was a tingle dying as quickly as it was felt, a barrier for the emerald mist which pressed against it in coiling plumes. Outside the area was clear air and Dumarest gulped at it, inflating his lungs, fighting a momentary dizziness. Drugs, subtle additions to the emerald steam which had triggered a latent violence. Why had he ever considered killing Zalman? There was no need for murder; lies, a pretended agreement and a later parting would have been enough. He had managed to elude the Cyclan—how much easier it would be to elude a man.

"Earl!" Zalman was at his side, his face strained. "You would have killed me."

There was no point in lying. "Yes."

"The mist. That damned mist." Zalman shuddered. "A hell of a place to hold a conference."

But one which others had found suitable for love. A labored breathing came from a bank of orange, a giggle from a plume of scarlet. From twists of ochre a man, naked, stepped toward Dumarest. Behind him a girl, adorned only with her hair, followed, smiling with drugged vacuousness.

"Him, Brill. Him!"

"The small one?"

"No, the big."

"As I thought." The man hadn't turned to look at his companion. "A wager," he said to Dumarest. "The girl against what? Have you money?"

Like the girl he was drugged, spoiling for combat, a man proud of his physical attributes. He moved to block the path as Dumarest stepped forward.

"We fight," he said. "You win and the girl is yours to use as you want. I win and you give me her value."

"Which is?"

"A year's labor at the standard rate."

More than the cost of a High passage and money he didn't have but the man gave Dumarest no time to argue. He attacked, cheered on by the girl, hands reaching, knee lifting in a savage jerk to the groin, head lowered and butting to break the nose and mash the lips over shattered teeth. An attack which vented itself on air as Dumarest moved aside.

"Coward!" Brill was annoyed. "Stand and fight like a man!"

He moved in again, this time kicking, his foot rising to slam forward, the heel aimed at the stomach. Dumarest caught it, twisted, threw the man off balance and staggering to one side. Purple vapor engulfed him and he

emerged snarling, followed by a woman with braided hair
who stood watching as the girl screamed encouragement.

"Get him, Brill! Hurt him! Show me blood!"

A bitch who would be as loyal to the man who won her
as she was to her present companion. She danced forward
with a suggestive thrust of the hips, a gyration of her buttocks which sent matching ripples up her torso and activated her small but pendulous breasts.

A distraction which Dumarest ignored. Brill was
drugged but the more dangerous because of that. Even
though unarmed his hands and feet could be used to
maim and kill. To underestimate an enemy was often the
last mistake a man made.

"Earl?" Zalman was concerned. "He means to kill
you."

"I know."

"Shall I help? No," he read the answer. "You don't
need me."

The next time Brill attacked Dumarest ceased being
gentle. He ducked, avoiding the fingers stabbing at his
eyes, the thumb hooked to rip at his mouth. Twisting he
guided the upthrusting knee from his testicles and then,
with cold deliberation, ended the conflict.

"Wonderful!" The woman with the braided hair clapped
her hands in admiration. "So neat! So fast! How often
did you hit him? Five times? Six?" She looked at the
limp figure sprawled unconscious on the tiles. "Will he
live?"

"Yes."

"Bruised and sore and he'll have no use for that chit
for awhile." She looked distastefully at the girl who stood,
simpering, waiting to be claimed. "But now, of course,
she is yours."

"Must I take her?"

"You will insult her if you don't but, no, there is no
obligation." She added, wistfully, "Had I been in her
place I could have wished there was."

"You flatter me, my lady."

"No, I am honest. But a word of warning. The man has
friends and wealthy relatives—need I say more?"

She had said enough and provided another reason for Dumarest to be on the move. Assassins were easy to hire and no man could stand against a powerful House. As he turned to leave the girl ran after him.

"What about me?"

"Stay and take care of your friend."

"You don't want me?" Shocked incredulity shone in her eyes. "You really mean it! You reject me? You dirty, stinking—" She broke off as Dumarest closed her mouth with his palm. As she twisted free her eyes glowed with a warped anticipation. "Are you going to beat me? Hurt me? Make me grovel? Are you? Are you?"

Zalman said, "Get dressed and wait for us outside. You have fifteen minutes."

They left the baths in three, Zalman leading the way to where a small park rested enclosed by plumed trees and adorned by a tinkling fountain. A bench rested in the seclusion of bushes and he sat looking up at Dumarest.

"Sit, Earl. We must talk."

About Earth and his claim.

"Of course. How shall I begin? With my knowledge of your interest? That I learned from Bochner who won the information from a woman you confided in. He thought as she must have done that you were bemused by a legend. Ask the next hundred people who pass you why if they know of the planet and they will tell you it does not exist. Earth is a world like Bonanza and Jackpot and El Dorado. Like Eden and Paradise and a place called Heaven. Realms born of wishful longings. Planets which hold all the things anyone could ever desire. And, if you insist and tell them the world does actually exist they will ask where are the coordinates?"

"You have them?"

"No." Zalman met his eyes. "I am honest with you, Earl. And you will not kill me. Not here. Not ever unless I cheat you and that will never be." He added, quickly. "No. I was not talking merely to save my life."

He read too much; from the expression on his face he had learned Dumarest's suspicions and he wondered who could ever tolerate such a man. The rounded face gave the answer. Zalman was alone. His talent had locked him in a prison of isolation.

He said, wistfully, "You are probably the first to realize that." Then, shaking his head, "Maybe I shouldn't have said that but I seem unable to remember my talent can be offensive."

"Only when you display it. If you waited before speaking you could manage to keep it hidden. Surely you have tried that?"

"Of course, but, Earl, can you imagine what it is to know the woman you love is lying when she tells you she is yours alone? Or to know a friend is betraying you? A companion plotting your destruction? To know you are being robbed and deluded and taken for all kinds of a fool? My own father—my mother—" He broke off, shaking his head. "I thought they would be pleased but how mistaken I was. Who would guess parents could be so cruel? You, perhaps, yes, I think you have no love for your childhood."

A time he preferred to forget. Dumarest said, "And Earth?"

"Exists. Or, at least, I know of a man who swears it does. I will take you to him and from him you may learn what it is you wish to know. My share of our agreement. Yours?"

"I have nothing you can use."

"So you say but I am convinced otherwise. Well, it can wait. I trust you. Later, after you have met the man I spoke of we will talk again." He rose, stretching, "Shall we go?"

"To where?"

"The field. To find a ship and book passage. The man you want is on Elysius."

Chapter THREE

Jarvet had anticipated reassignment but was not surprised when retained. Nequal had molded the apex of his world to his own design and the new Cyber Prime would have found the fit not wholly to his liking. The diet, for example; Nequal had been old, his body able to maintain itself on little, but Elge needed more calories to keep his metabolism at an optimum level. The same with the temperature of his new quarters which he found too high, their illumination which he found too bright, and alterations were needed in the schedule which had been geared to his predecessor's biological clock. Small things but more efficiently dealt with by an experienced aide than one new to the position and Jarvet had not served Nequal long enough to have been strictured by his routine.

Elge checked a report and added it to a pile before looking at the man where he stood beyond the desk. The Elmay situation had been dealt with and a new disposition of cybers made in the Phalange Confederation. More work remained but he sensed the aide wanted his attention.

"Yes?"

"Master, those for processing wait in the reception chamber."

Cybers, old, ill, some diseased but all retaining clarity of mind and now ready to receive their earned reward. Custom dictated they be welcomed and addressed by the Cyber Prime; a tradition far from an empty formality. Minds reassured by personal contact gained added strength of determination and were better fitted to withstand the psychic shock of transference.

"How many? Four? When are the next expected?"

"Five will be arriving the day after tomorrow."

Why not save those present until then and greet them all at the same time? Work halved and time saved—yet would it be efficient? Elge decided not; the surgeons would be ready with their assistants and apparatus and the saving of his own effort would be lost in the waste of their greater potential. Also it took time to complete the processing and to work them too hard and under pressure would be to create unnecessary strain. Even so the facets of the situation had to be examined.

"Prepare an update on operation schedules with particular reference to transference processing based on the use of latest equipment together with any probable advantages to be gained by new techniques."

A minute gained by the use of an added machine would make that inclusion worthwhile. The same amount of time lost by the release of an assistant would pay in dividends gained by the saving of labor. The objective of the Cyber Prime as Jarvet had quickly learned; to maximize potential and minimize waste. Even efficiency was a matter of degree and Elge was a new broom intent on sweeping clean.

Jarvet said, "Will you decide on the Thailen Disposition now, Master?"

He watched as Elge studied the data. A man as intent as Nequal had been but one with a different background. Not for him the slums and lucky chance of winning the attention of the Cyclan. Elge was of the minority and held an advantage most lacked. The younger son of a wealthy House, a strange, tormented boy who had found an escape in books and a pride in mental achievement. One who had a father with the foresight to recognize an advantage but lacked the understanding to see how futile his ambition was. A cyber recognized no family, no friends, no allegiance other than to the organization of which he was a part. Once accepted he lost his past, his very name, and the operation performed at puberty rid him of all emotion including the possibility of regret.

Facts which had won the Cyclan a dedicated servant and had cost a father his youngest son.

One who now pondered the destruction of a world.

Subtlety was taking too long to resolve the problem; the cabal ruling the Thailen Disposition was entrenched and stubborn. Greed, the natural ally of the Cyclan, was a tool which had a blunted edge as was ambition and hope. The Disposition had been designed by an expert in human behavior and the pattern he had formed a century ago still held strength. But all such societies were brittle and, like glass, would shatter if the correct force could be determined.

Within seconds Elge had decided what that force must be.

Rising he activated the galactic depiction and adjusted the relevant sector. The worlds of the Disposition were close; Thailen marked with green, the two others in yellow and blue. Planets united in a mutual dependency, self-sufficient, a barrier to the domination of the Cyclan.

One to be broken by the use of plague. A mutated virus introduced to Thailen would decimate the population and spread an enervating weakness through the survivors. Mutual aid had its limits; soon resentments and irritations would become manifest—emotions exacerbated by skilled agents and contrived situations leading to violent incidents. Thailen, deserted by its allies, would be forced to appeal to the Cyclan for help in order to survive. The rest would be simply a matter of time.

Jarvet said, "Which virus, Master?"

"HXT 3274." A product of the Cyclan laboratories and kept well away from the complex in which he stood as were all such compounds. "Prepare relevant schedules."

Times, costs in terms of material and labor, relative efficiencies—such a plan must not be allowed to fail. And it was one beyond the normal scope of operations—the Cyclan had no need to wage such outright if hidden war. Was Elge impatient to make his reputation? A thought

Jarvet dismissed as soon as formed; such small ambition would have eradicated him from the organization long ago. What then? A desire to advance the major ideal? To demonstrate to the Council that they had been correct in having chosen him to take Nequal's place?

Without looking at the aide Elge said, "You think I am using excessive force to solve the problem. That it is a demonstration of misplaced zeal."

Statements, not questions, and Jarvet recognized the trap. To agree was to tell his superior that he thought him less than he should be. To deny was to betray a weakness—no cyber should ever be awed by rank when the one holding it had shown a lack of efficiency. A dilemma from which Elge saved him.

"Observe." The depiction expanded still farther to show the area in fine detail. "Kochbar, close to the Thailen Disposition and one still to accept the services we offer. They are skilled in the manufacture of biological compounds and provide growth-stimulators to the farmers of Thailen. Once the plague has been introduced the order of probability of them being blamed is eighty-three percent."

Other customers would cancel their orders, the industry would suffer, poverty move in and the economy shatter—dangerous pressures for a ruling class operating on a feudal system. It was almost certain that one or more of the great Houses would call on the Cyclan for aid. The advice the cybers gave, the subtle influence they would bring to bear, and another world would shine scarlet in the depiction.

And yet was even the winning of worlds worth the waste inherent in the means to be employed?

Again Elge answered his unspoken question.

"HXT 3274 has yet to be tested on a wide scale and much can be learned from an actual field-application. Also it is a virus allied to the emotional content of the victim in that it responds to the level of adrenaline and tension generated in the thalamus. There will be waste, yes, and that is to be deplored, but the victims will be mostly from types with a high emotional content."

Dreamers, idealists, those who hated the cold efficiency of applied logic and who would be natural enemies of the Cyclan. Once they had been eliminated the rest would be relatively simple. Waste in terms of potential labor and active units, yes, but set against the greater gain it was minimal.

Jarvet looked at Elge with a new respect. Already the man had shown his ability to grasp more than just the immediate pattern. The situation had helped, naturally, but he had been quick to realize its full potential and to determine the best means to employ. Yet the naked use of power was a drug and he must be watched to ensure he did not rely on it too strongly. As Nequal had been watched and finally condemned for his failure. His inability to master a single man. Would Elge succeed where he had failed?

Someone in the salon was singing: a simple melody of five repetitive notes, the lilt accompanied by the twanging of a stringed instrument; a performance which could have normally held a certain charm but which was only an irritating noise. Dumarest was glad when it ceased and was replaced by the usual sounds to be found on any ship in space: the transmitted vibration of voices, movement, the hum of the Earhaft drive which whispered from the very fabric of the vessel and told that all was well.

Lying supine on the bunk he stared at the roof of the cabin he shared with Zalman. The man was absent but his presence remained as a subtle something in the atmosphere; the hint of body odor, the pomade he used on his hair, the tang of lotions, the fluids used to clean his garments. Things normally unnoticed but Dumarest had brought them to the forefront of his consciousness; scents he tested like an animal and found innocent.

Yet questions remained.

Coincidences happened as Zalman had pointed out; his meeting with Bochner, his being on the same world at the same time as Dumarest, his knowing of a man who knew the whereabouts of Earth. All could be pure coincidence—but so many and so complementary?

The music began again, this time a low, humming croon which merged with and accentuated the vibration of the drive, the throb of strings adding an extra dimension. Dumarest tried to guess who the singer could be; Julie Dimault, the fading woman with the gilded hair? Estelle Lamont, young but aged with a peculiar blight? Sven Axilia the tough miner with scarred hands and a face frozen into a perpetual sneer? Ochen? Quail? Tocsaw? Rosichien? Marriol?

A minor problem and Dumarest dismissed it as he looked at the smeared paint of the roof. The *Phril* had little to commend it. The third vessel they had taken after leaving Lyten and the last he could afford. Elysius was not the easiest place to reach.

Yet, if it held a man who knew where Earth was to be found then he must go there. He had no other choice.

Again the music ended and Dumarest rose, stretching, passing from the cabin into the passage leading to the salon. The singer had been Estelle who sat now with her eyes staring vacantly before her, the stringed instrument on her lap, held by lax fingers. A cheap thing as her gown was cheap, the gilded ring she wore, the faded bloom in her hair. An artificial depiction of a natural glory now dulled and eroded by time. And yet the girl herself was young as the lines of her body and the firmness of her skin betrayed.

As Julie Dimault was old.

She smiled from where she sat at the table, hard eyes matched by the brittle glow of gems, the gold gleaming from her tresses. A woman who had lived and loved and now flaunted her possessions like a banner of defiance. One faded as the flower in the girl's hair was faded but from a far different cause.

"Earl, come and join us!" Ochen extended the invitation, turning in his chair, rolls of fat gathering beneath his chin. "Maybe you'll change my luck."

"You need skill, not luck." Rosichien was sour. "Top price for a High passage and we get skinned on the journey too. To hell with it!"

He rose, throwing down his cards, leaving the salon to

head for his cabin, his bunk, the compounds he carried in his bag and which would yield him erotic dreams. Watching him go Tocsaw said, thoughtfully, "He has a point."

"You think I am robbing you? Cheating?" Like all such ships the *Phril* carried a man to work the table; a gambler who was paid with a share of the profits he made. Now Chamdo looked at the assembly. "If you want to change the game I am willing. The cards too—you can even ask one of your number to deal."

A wild suggestion—how could he hope to use his skill if it was accepted? Yet did he need to cheat? Dumarest, from his own experience, decided it would be unnecessary. The players were too inexperienced and the gambler too proficient as he must have discovered during the journey. The offer had been an empty gesture.

Zalman said, "Some men are bad losers and we've just lost the company of one of them. Well, it's small loss. Like to take his place, Earl?"

"That's right, sit down and let's get on with the game." Julie glared at the dealer. "Come on, man, let's get on with it. I've lost too much to quit now."

A claim Zalman couldn't make. The table before him was heavy with money and Dumarest could guess how he'd got it. It took little skill to win if you could read from your opponents what they held.

"You joining?" Chambo waited, cards poised to deal. As Dumarest took the chair he added, "Good. Let's see your money."

The game was spectrum; seven cards to a hand, two draws of up to five a time. A full rainbow was the top hand with various combinations of colors forming different values. A basically simple game but one allowing for wild betting and the use of bluff. Dumarest played with caution, using his limited resources to back only good hands and not trying to buck impossible odds. A system which had doubled his wealth when, after a couple of hours, Julie flung down her cards.

"That's enough!" She scowled as Zalman drew in the

E. C. Tubb

pot. "Four violets and three reds and still I lose. Talk about luck! I've lots of it—all bad!"

"Me too!" Like the woman Ochen had had enough. "How about you, Sven?"

Chambo shrugged as the miner shook his head. "You want to change the game? Poker? Starsmash? High, low, man-in-between? No?" He rose, yawning, "Well, that's me for now. I need to get some sleep. You want to play on just help yourself." His gesture included the cards, the table, "Have fun."

"The bastard!" Julie snatched at the cards and began to examine them. "Was he cheating, Earl?"

"He didn't have to cheat."

"But was he?"

"No." Dumarest smiled as the woman looked for nicked edges, marks, frays or any sign the cards had been fixed. "He's a professional," he explained. "His living depends on being able to outguess you, outbluff you and outplay you."

"What about him?" She glanced at Zalman. "And you didn't lose either."

"I'm lucky," said Zalman. "Earl is just clever."

"He's more than that." Her eyes held admiration. "He's the kind of man a woman would leave home for. Work for too, if he asked her." She was blunt with a directness he recognized. "Look me up after we land. If you want work I could use you. A house always needs someone to handle trouble should it walk through the door." She frowned at Zalman, his smile. "Something amusing you?"

"You ever been to Elysius before?"

"No, why?"

"Take some advice. If you're thinking of opening a house you'd do better to move on with the ship."

"Competition?" Her face grew hard, ugly. "You talking about competition? Mister, I can handle that as I've done before. If you're trying to warn me off forget it."

"I'm trying to help. You don't know the situation."

"Like hell I don't! Sure, this is my first visit, but you think I'm a fool?" Julie nodded to where the girl sat like a child with her toy instrument in her lap. "Where do you think I found her? You want to know about Elysius she's the one to tell you. She was born there."

The wine had been watered until it was almost a ghost but enough flavor remained to mask the taste of the stimulant it contained. Dumarest knelt before her, the glass in his hand, forcing himself on her attention.

"Here!" He thrust the glass into her hand. "Drink. I want you to drink!"

"Drink?" Her voice was as empty as her eyes. "You want me to drink?"

"Yes." He was patient. "Take a sip and then a swallow. Then another sip and another swallow." Her throat moved in mechanical obedience. "That's it. Now finish the rest."

They were almost alone in the salon. Julie Dimault had been escorted to her cabin by Zalman who had read Dumarest's intention. The others had followed the gambler to their bunks. Only the miner remained, sitting at the table, brooding, sipping at wine.

"Better?" Dumarest took away the empty glass. Soon the drugs would lend her strength to break the shell around her. "How about some music?"

A mistake—how often had she been asked to play? He sensed her recoil, the withdrawal into herself; the warm, snug, private place in which no one could touch her, none do her harm. He said, quietly, "Talk to me, Estelle. Tell me about your home. About Elysius."

For answer she touched the strings of the instrument lying in her lap. Sound rose, whining, breaking into a glissade, a ripple, to whine again as if in pain. The answer which could have been given by a mute but he had heard her sing.

"Elysius," he said again. "Estelle, tell me of your home."

From the table Sven Axilia said, "You waste your time and what could she say? To her home was a place from which to run."

As it had been to him?

Dumarest said, without turning, "Don't interfere. Just drink your wine."

"Drink and listen to a fool? It needs an urge from the harridan to bring the girl to her senses. I watched as she persuaded her to sing—God knows why. Who wants to hear such caterwauling?" Wine gurgled as he refilled his glass. "Women! Trouble every last damned one of them. Like the bitch who threw acid in my face. She aimed for the eyes but I caught the glint of light on the moving vial and took it on the cheek instead. Now, each time I look into a mirror I see the reason to curse the whole stinking sex."

He stood, swaying, catching at the table to steady himself, sending wine to flood from the bottle he'd knocked on its side. He stared at it for a moment then cursed and headed toward the door. As he vanished Dumarest drew his knife.

"Estelle!" The light flared in sudden brilliance from the polished steel. A gleam which he directed at her eyes. "Estelle!"

The girl could be conditioned and from what the miner had said he guessed she was. A precaution against her saying too much? One designed to keep her submissive? Julie, wise in the ways of her trade, would know about such things.

"Estelle, listen to me." The knife moved, brilliance illuminating the empty, staring eyes. "You are waking up now. You are waking up. You want to stand and talk and laugh. Wake up, girl! Wake!"

"What time is it?" Her voice had the thin quality of a child or a woman who had grown too fast. "Is it time yet? Have we arrived? Do you want me to sing? I am good at singing."

"And what else?"

"I can dance a little. And cook. And sew." Her voice deepened as if she had suddenly become aware of his face, the knife he held. "What is this? Who are you? What the hell are you doing?"

"Asking questions." He lowered the blade and sheathed it within his boot. "Just talking. Feel better now?"

"Was I bad?"

"Giddy," he lied. "A little dizzy. I gave you a drink. Have you known Julie long?"

"No."

"But you're traveling with her, right?" At her nod he said, "To Elysius? Your home world?" He waited until again she had nodded. "Why?"

"Business. Our business."

One he could guess. He rose to look down at her, at the cheap tinsel finery, the young face marred with lines which did not belong. A runaway who had found hell where she'd hoped to find heaven. A girl who could be at war with herself; one subject to sudden, maniacal rages or suicidal frenzies—was that why she had been conditioned?

He said, gently, "You have a family? Parents? A sister, perhaps?" Her answer was short and what he'd expected. She flinched as he lifted his hand but he used it only to tilt back her chin. "You don't have to be afraid of me, girl. I mean you no harm. Why don't you tell me about yourself? Your family?"

For a moment he thought he'd won then the doors closed behind her eyes and the young face regained its blighted mask. She could be answering but if so it was in a manner only Zalman could understand.

"Earl!" He stood at the door looking into the salon. His face cleared as Dumarest turned and walked toward him. "Still here? I thought—"

"No."

"But—"

"You were wrong." It made a change for him to read the other man. "I only wanted to talk to her."

"And you had no luck."

"No. Where's Julie?"

"Doped and sleeping." Disgust edged Zalman's voice. "The old hag! She did nothing but complain about her luck and left me in no doubt she would have preferred your company to mine. A chance there, Earl, if you've a mind to take it. You could win more than her affection; those gems she wears are genuine and she has a shrewd sense of business." He glanced to where the girl was again sitting, eyes vacuous, the stringed instrument in her hands. "But it seems you have no liking for what she has to sell."

"I want you to buy her."

"Estelle? But—"

"Buy her." Dumarest explained, patiently, "Julie lost heavily at cards and will be eager to recoup her losses. Hint that the girl has conned her and will be a liability. Do it right and you'll get her cheap." He added, "And do it soon—we land tomorrow."

Chapter FOUR

———◆◦◆———

The blood had gone, the flesh, the skin, the bone—all reduced to basic elements and distributed for use as fertilizer. Only the brain remained and that was important only because it provided the receptacle which housed the mind; the burning intelligence which distinguished humans from beasts and which alone could solve the secrets of the universe. A brain now sealed and enclosed; a mass of convoluted tissue little larger than a pair of clenched fists.

All that remained of Nequal, the recent Cyber Prime.

"Waking has been delayed," said Icelus. "Extended five days beyond the normal period in order to minimize any traumas induced by the unusual situation. The element of primeval fear cannot be ignored in the presence of doubt introduced by the possible limitation of continued survival."

The maximizing of potential—Elge agreed with the procedure. But to wait longer would be to wait for no useful purpose.

"Has everything been checked and tested?" To ask was to insult the engineers but he had to be certain. "All attachments made?"

"Linkage is with the affected unit only," said Icelus. "There is, and will be, no contact with Central Intelligence at this time. Electronic apparatus will provide for monitoring and communication."

Machines to alter the flow of nutrients, to change the temperature, adjust ionic balance, to take the cerebral stimulus and relay it through meters, dials, speakers.

41

More confusions added to those expected by a brain divorced from its natural housing. One now sleeping from the effects of microcurrents fed directly into the sleep center of the brain.

A touch and it would wake—to face what?

Elge had tried to imagine it, closing his eyes, dulling his senses, drifting in a void of sensory deprivation but it could never be the same. Not even when the Homochon elements had been activated by the Samatchazi formulae and rapport had been achieved with the massed brains could a cyber know just what it must be like to be finally rid of the irritation of flesh. When in communication there was an engulfing, an absorption of knowledge as if it had been water sucked from the mind by a sponge. Data taken and instructions given in near-instantaneous exchange against which the speed of light was a crawl. And, afterward, when the rapport was broken and the Homochon elements turned toward quiescence, came the period of mental exultation in which the entire universe was filled with the glowing light of alien intelligences.

Would Nequal enjoy that pleasure in unbroken munificence? Would he even remember the reason for his having been processed?

"Master?" Icelus was waiting. "We can maintain the present status for another thirty hours if necessary but to wait longer would be to invite deterioration of the psyche."

Time—why was there so little of it? Even by cutting his hours of rest there was not enough and to do with less was to endanger the optimum working of his body and a consequent dulling of his mind. A matter to be investigated—why did men need to sleep? If a substitute could be found, a drug or mental discipline, how much more efficient they would be.

A thing he would look into but now Icelus was waiting his decision.

"Now!"

Immediately Nequal was awake.

It was an awakening without sight, without feeling, like

a man rising from sleep yet still locked in drowsiness, still clinging to the surrogate womb of comfort and oblivion. Awake and tasting the dissolving fragments of dreams. Seeing flashes of color and pictures which were items composed of assorted trifles; places, faces, incidents—a montage constructed of memories. Cybers he had known; Yandron, Quendis, Wain—his early instructors, the companions of his youth, the rulers he had advised. Almost a century of accumulated data presented in wild disarray; a jumble of misplaced times and situations, a melange of events.

"Initial disturbance nearing climax," said Icelus, looking at his instruments. "The peak is as expected."

Madness!

He tried to scream but found he had no mouth. To see but discovered he had no eyes. To hear to find only silence. To move, to feel, to discover both impossible. He could only think, to be aware, to know what had happened and what he now was.

Gladness!

Now he could rest and, free of all pressures, probe abstract concepts. Light blazed in mental brilliance, forming equations which he held with a part of his attention while he expanded them with others, the equations changing, altering at a thought, a little blurred as yet but time and practice would cure that as it would his present euphoria.

A city rose on a plain, each item clearly marked, the inner structure plain, the molding of the segments, the fittings of joints, the foundations, the power sources, the water, the waste disposal—all built with mental imagery. And this was just play. Next would come the abtruse construction of a system of pure mathematics, the selection of a particular problem in multi-dimensional geometry or an investigation into the properties of inert matter.

"The unit has successfully peaked," reported Icelus. "The curve is following the normal pattern but continued isolation could create variables it would be better to avoid."

Time for another decision.

"Engage." Elge watched the bank of instruments. "Complete."

A dial moved—Nequal was no longer alone.

Isobel stirred, reluctant to wake, hugging the memory of a dream before opening her eyes. It was late, the window bright with luminescence, yet the house was strangely silent and the bedside table lacked her morning cup of tisane. A silence broken by the jar of the phone as she rose and left the bedroom naked but for a robe. She ignored the instrument; other things came first and whoever was calling could call again. The musical tone ceased as she searched the house.

The servants were gone; her maid, the cook, the two cleaners, the mechanic who serviced the raft. The vehicle itself had not been loaded which added to her irritation. An emotion she fought as she returned to the bedroom—on Elysius anger was futile.

The phone rang again as she showered, again as she made a simple breakfast. Mtouba, the Hausi, stared at her from the screen.

"Madam Boulaye—I was beginning to think something was wrong."

"Because I didn't answer?" She forced herself to smile. "Sorry, but it's one of those days. You understand."

Too well, but his face, scarred with caste marks livid against the chocolate of his skin, remained the bland visage of an idol. A man firm in his niche and in control of his environment. She could almost envy the agent.

He said, "At least you are well and I am glad to hear it. I called to see if you wished to add anything to your shipment or to give me any instructions as regards supplies. The *Phril* is due to arrive later today and it would be unwise to miss the opportunity."

"Thank you for letting me know."

"You have nothing to add?"

"Sorry, Mtouba, you have it all."

"All?" She sensed his disapproval. "I'd hoped for better news. You realize, of course, that what I hold will barely pay for the supplies delivered on your order? I am reluctant to mention it but your credit is almost totally exhausted."

Did he think her unable to calculate? "I am aware of the position, but surely you appreciate my difficulties? The juscar is available and I know it. What you hold is proof of that—the only difficulty at the moment is in getting it out. And I'm not without security."

"Your deed?"

"Naturally."

"You have assets on some other world?" He knew the answer before she shook her head. "A pity. The deed you hold on the Fulda Hills is, to be blunt—"

"Worthless." She said it for him. "But I have other things. Don't worry, Mtouba, I'll make out."

"I'm certain of it." He smiled, ending the conversation. "I wish you luck, Madam Boulaye."

A cheap wish—what she needed were men of determination to tear free the wealth lying in the hills. The metal was there as Rudi had sworn but not even he had guessed how hard it would be to obtain.

Memory of him soured the taste of the food and she pushed aside the barely touched breakfast to sip at a cup of spiced tisane. Rudi who had loved her and whom she had loved though he had been twenty years her senior. A man with an intellect she had admired yet one tainted with a streak of romanticism which had finally cost him his life. A trait to which she had responded at first, finding herself stimulated by his flights of imaginative speculation. They'd married and he had wanted to give her the universe to adorn her beauty. Now he was dead and she was alone.

Like the food the tisane tasted sour and she rose from the table with sudden impatience. It was a waste of time but again she searched the house finding it as deserted as before. For a moment she debated as to whether or not to load the raft then decided against it. To fly to the hills would be a wasted journey. Instead she climbed to the roof.

Over the hills the devils were dancing.

They rose high against the sky to the east, thick plumes

which spread like smoke from distant explosions to be caught and shaped by the wind into a series of new and elaborate configurations; men, beasts, demons, creatures from delirium. Puffs of yellow and green, scarlet and orange, amber and dusty brown all starkly clear against the pale azure of the sky. A long line of them dancing above the Fulda Hills.

Rudi had given them their name as they had stood watching on the flat roof, his arm around her, his body close. She could visualize it now, the gray hair fluttering, his thin, peaked face alive with interest, one hand lifted, pointing as if he were giving a lecture back at the university where once he had taught and she had studied.

Devils—they were well-named. They had taken his life.

She felt the sting of tears and the sudden wetness of her cheeks. He had tried too hard, attempted too much and she had remained silent when she should have objected. The lure of wealth, the promise of a fortune—how could she have been such a fool? Why hadn't they realized that there had to be something wrong?

The wind strengthened a little, drying the tears on her cheeks but more followed born of the memory she couldn't forget. The scream, the rumble, the sudden fall and, as the dust settled, the sight of the body lying half buried, limp, the face turned toward her, one hand extended as if in mute appeal. A hand which held a scrap of metal, the juscar for which he'd given his life. His last gift to her—a fraction of what he'd intended.

A scrap of metal and a name.

The devils increased even as she watched, fresh puffs rising to join the others, compact masses of color to replace the thinning clouds. The swarms bred and nurtured in domes which swelled to grow taut from internal pressures to rip apart in final dissolution. From them, blasted by expanding vapors, the spore-like ephemerae rose high to be caught by the winds, to wheel and spin in a mating frenzy. The males, having vented their seed, would perish to drift dead and drying on the winds. The females, gravid, would spread to select new sites for fresh colonies.

Had the devils danced when Rudi had died? She couldn't remember but, if she had been a little earlier, she would have been with him. Impatient he had gone on ahead, turning to shout to her to hurry, a shout which could have caused the fall.

Now he was buried, the devils his only memorial.

From where he sat at the console Icelus said, "A node, Master. Termination of coherent thought now unmistakable. Uniting the brains has not achieved the desired result."

A failure and one Elge was reluctant to accept. "Increase the cerebral stimulus to level five."

Pain was the product of stimulation of the appropriate center of the brain and was a tool he did not hesitate to use. From the speakers came a thresh of sound; a keening breaking into a shriek which died as the microcurrents were cut.

"Reading?"

"Previous conclusion verified."

As was the failure, and the blame had to be his: Elge assessed it as he faced the console. It had been his decision to accept Nequal's offer and the reward could have been great. As it was, time and effort had been used to no purpose. Nequal would die and the affected unit would be destroyed at the same time. And yet, surely, something must have been learned?

"Replay the recording," he ordered. "Revised version."

One which eliminated all unessential data and yet was still not easy to understand. The confusing jumble of electronically translated "noise" was gone but other confusions remained. Words, sounds, crackles—how inefficient mechanical devices were when compared to the interplay of intelligent minds.

"Master?"

"Begin. Open speakers.

Let them all hear there was nothing to hide and someone in the room could catch a significance he might miss. Elge leaned forward, concentrating, imagining himself to have been in Nequal's position when the linkage was established. There would have been a moment of doubt, a questing, a reminder of the original purpose, then a sudden awareness of company.

Why had it sent him mad?

He tried to find the answer in the blurring susurration of sound. A voice, calling, another answering with tears. A question followed by others and insistance through repetition. Normal therapy and practice and what he would have expected but Elge knew that more had happened than had been recorded. A change of viewpoint, perhaps? An altered framework of reference? A distortion of familiar reality or the sudden awareness of a truth so disturbing that the mind had found escape in mania?

Could such a truth exist?

Logically it could and he listened with an added interest even as a part of his mind examined the probabilities of what kind of truth it must be. A moment then he recognized the paradox; no truth determined by an intelligent mind could have the power to destroy that mind. A superstition, then? Could any cyber be so prone to error?

Yet Itel was no longer a cyber. His mind had retreated to a point long before he'd been accepted and given a new name. A child was subject to terrors and fears of darkness—had Nequal been affected by the power of unrestrained fantasies?

A shadow cast by a flying insect was, to a child, a shapeless monster of horrific dimensions. A whisper in darkness which, to a man would be a trick of acoustics, was to a young and impressionable mind the murmuring of an alien hungry for flesh. Vampires, ghouls, ghosts, and goblins—all creatures born of imagination and ignorance as were witches and sorcerers. Yet more than one planet had seen the smoke of their burning.

And, if a trained and sharpened mind could be affected by childish terrors wouldn't the impact be proportionally great?

A possibility Elge pondered as he listened to the recording. Nequal was whimpering now, pleading, a drone broken by a sudden scream as stimulus had been applied to jerk him back to an awareness of his mission. Had that induced agony added to his confusion?

The recording ended to be followed by silence. One broken as Icelus said, "Something may be learned if I plot present electroencephalograms with previous recordings. I could be mistaken but it seemed that not only Itel but Nequal himself was displaying signs of extreme emotion."

To be expected in a child. A concept alien to a cyber.

"Regression?"

"Apparently so."

"Contaminated by the affected unit?"

"The probability is of the order of ninety-seven percent." Icelus glanced at the others present; his aides, technicians. "Perhaps someone has something to add?"

A technician said, "With permission I would like to conduct an experiment."

"With the affected units?"

"Those together with the recordings. There could be information in the material we have eliminated from the version just heard. While, to us, it seems to be merely noise yet it must hold within itself some code value to those originating it. It might be possible to use that code value to stimulate an automatic response."

As a man would flinch at a scream or respond to an ingrained conditioning at a signal. The idea held merit.

Elge said, "How would you attempt to translate a response if received?"

"Electronic comparison, Master. We can itemize all signals and break each down into fractionated particles. A code, by definition, must be repetitive and it should be possible to match, isolate, and reassemble to achieve a comprehensive result. It will take time and the probability of success is low; of the order of eighteen percent."

Low indeed but little would be lost by trying.

"I agree." Elge rose from his chair. "Let me know immediately when you have a conclusive result."

It came fifteen hours later after he had woken from a brief sleep to study reports from a dozen worlds. It was short—a single word. Elysius.

Chapter FIVE

There was no gate, no fence, no guards. The field was nothing but a bare expanse of dirt edged to the north with rambling buildings which could have been warehouses. The town sprawled on the slope behind them, a ramshackle collection of dwellings parted by winding roads. To the south the valley widened as it headed toward the distant ocean.

"Home," said Estelle. "Welcome to Elysius."

Her tone was bitter and Dumarest could guess why. She had slept and bathed and had discarded her cheap finery and now looked clean and neat but the improvement since had been small. She was still withdrawn, still masked and aged with a peculiar blight.

Dumarest looked again at the town not liking what he saw. The signs were familiar and he could guess why the girl had run. The planet was at the end of the line, a dead-end world lacking industry or even a viable agriculture. One without opportunity for a man to find himself work and build a stake so as to buy passage and move on. The worst kind of landing for any traveler. Once stranded it was too easy to starve.

"Not here, Earl." Zalman seemed amused. "There's no fear of that here."

"That's nice to know. Why didn't you tell me?"

"Why? Would it have made any difference?" He looked at the sky, the sun reaching for the horizon. "We'd better find somewhere to stay."

There was no hurry. Dumarest turned and looked at where the *Phril* was resting. The handler, steward, gam-

50

bler and a Hausi had loaded it and now it was ready to
leave. Julie had stayed aboard, moving on with Rosichien
and Marriol, and he wondered if, even now, she was
laughing. As far as he could tell no passengers had been
waiting to embark.

"There rarely are," said Zalman. "People come but not
many want to leave. That's the charm of this place."

One Dumarest found hard to understand. The town
held the unmistakable atmosphere of a slum but, while
the buildings were delapidated, he could see none of the
usual abject poverty. The edge of the field was free of
beggars, harlots, maimed children set to arouse a transient
pity. Even the usual sightseers who came to study the new
arrivals were absent.

"A hell of a place." Sven Axilia, scowling, spat in the
dirt. "I heard there was mining here, a big operation. One
day I'll meet up with the cheat who sold me the lie."

"You came to work?" Ochen grinned and shook his
head. "Man, why be a fool? You don't need to work on
Elysius. Right, Jon?"

"That's what I heard." Quail drew in his breath. "Well,
let's find somewhere to sit. Get some decent food too,
maybe. You coming with us?"

Tocsaw grunted. "Might as well."

"You?" Quail looked at Dumarest. "I guess not." His
eyes fell to the girl. "Well, have fun."

"Some people take chances," murmured Zalman as the
group moved away. "But I'm glad you didn't decide to
take offense. But about the girl—what happens now?"

"Do you need me to tell you?"

"No, but I'm taking your advice. To wait and let others
tell me what I already know. The Hausi, naturally."

"What else?" Dumarest added, dryly, "Who better to
know how to find her family. You're doing well, Hans."

Better than himself. The girl could have run from poverty in which case she wouldn't be welcome but, if nothing else, the purchase had gained her freedom of choice.
Mtouba ended the doubts.

He met them in his office at the edge of the field, a
small room stacked with files and samples, the air redo-

lent with the scent of pungent spices, perfumes, dried fruits, vials of dusts. He leaned back in his chair and looked up at the girl.

"Estelle Lamont." His eyes moved to Dumarest. "It was kind of you to bring her back."

"You know her?"

"I know her family. They have an estate to the west. Her father is dead now but there is an older sister and others. If you wish I will contact them."

He would do it anyway. Dumarest said, "Just tell them the girl is here. Will they come in to pick her up?"

"Not today. Haven't you seen the sky? It is full of color—but I forget, you are strangers. Can you keep her with you? Tomorrow I may be able to arrange transportation. Within a few days she will be safely home."

"A few days?"

"I will do the best I can." The agent spread his hands in a gesture symbolic of his limitations. "It is a matter of time, you understand. A bad period, to be sure, as to what can and cannot be accomplished but I promise to do what I can. Just be a little patient. Have you anywhere to stay? No? In that case I would recommend the Argive House. The owner is a woman of culinary skill and is exceptionally fastidious. Also," again he looked at the girl, "she has an appreciation of certain situations."

"Earl!" Zalman was quick. "He doesn't mean it the way it sounds."

The man was too sensitive. Dumarest said, "Where do I find this paragon?"

She was like her tavern, tall, wide, pleasing to look at. She came to meet them, smiling, hands lifted in a gesture of greeting. "Welcome to the Argive House" Her eyes measured each in turn, came to rest on Dumarest. "I am Anna Sefton. You?" Her smile broadened. "Earl! I like the name! You will be staying long?"

"A day, maybe a few days, it depends."

"On what? The girl?" She looked at Estelle who had said nothing. "Is she—do you want her to share your room? Or would you prefer me to take care of her? She has been away too long as you probably realize and needs help."

"Can you give it?"

"Of course." Her laughter was a warm contralto. "How stupid we are at times! If nothing else I have learned the necessity for discretion and yet who can tell another's customs? If my assumption offended you I apologize."

"There's no need." Dumarest, grateful for her help, smiled back. "Do you run this place on your own?"

"I own it and use what help I can get. Yours, I hope. If you have no business here on Elysius I would appreciate the offer of first refusal. Bed, board, all you can drink, and your choice of any girl—none would refuse you. At the end of six months the cost of a Low passage. That is if you are still interested."

"Who wouldn't be?"

"My last worker. I liked him, we became lovers, but even that wasn't enough. He stayed two months and followed the rest. Well, I have the consolation of knowing he doesn't suffer." She blinked then remembered her guests, the need to smile. "Celia!" The girl was obviously her daughter. "Show these gentlemen to room 15 while I take care of their lady." To Dumarest she added, "Dinner will be ready in an hour."

The room was large, the floor solid, the walls made of stone faced by inner panels of stained, smoothed, and polished wood. The windows were glazed with tinted glass with heavy curtains giving a barrier against the light. Twin beds rested wide apart and small tables, chairs and cabinets completed the furnishings.

Zalman said, "I didn't interfere down there, Earl, but if you'd rather have a room on your own just say the word."

He was practicing, being polite. Dumarest said, "This will do. Unless, of course, you prefer another arrangement."

While together he could watch the man—did Zalman have the same idea? As he shook his head Dumarest moved to examine the room. Though strongly built it showed signs of neglect; the panels could have done with wax, the curtains showed a minor rip, the tinted glass needed a few new panes to replace those cracked. The beds gave no cause for complaint. A drawer of a table held a scatter of old leaves, another some sheets of paper bearing odd scribbles. One of the chairs needed repairs to the seat.

A pattern continued outside. Dumarest leaned from the window to study the external walls, noting spots needing fresh mortar, others showing the effects of attrition. Reaching up he could touch the eaves and guessed the gutters would be full of sediment. A good house slowly going to ruin. He remembered the delapidation of the town.

"No workers, Earl." It took no talent to know what he must be thinking. "You heard the woman—bed, board, all you can drink and the rest of it. A snug berth for any traveler and a dream come true for a stranded one. I told you there was no danger of starving on Elysius."

One of the few things Zalman had mentioned and then only after they had landed. What other surprises was he holding in reserve?

The throb of a gong echoed from below as Dumarest left the bathroom where he had showered. Zalman had gone ahead and waved as Dumarest entered the dining room. It was long, low, set with tables and flanked at one end with a bar. Some drinkers stood there, mostly young, some wearing bright colors. A few girls similarly attired were among them. A normal assembly in any tavern but the place was too empty for its size.

"Hi!" Fitz Ochen nodded from where he sat. The others were with him. "Seems this is the best place in town. Where's Estelle?"

"Snug." Quail had been drinking. "Tucked away in a big, soft bed and waiting for her master. You did well there, Earl. If you want to pass her on I'm interested."

"In what?" Dumarest looked at him. "Buying her? You want to buy her?"

"No." Tocsaw spoke before Quail could answer; a man quick to end an impending quarrel. "He hasn't money enough. None of us have." Changing the subject he said, "Have any luck, Sven?"

The miner shook his head. "Not so far. If there's a mining operation on this world it has to be a small one. No equipment that I could see, no workers, none of what you'd expect."

Zalman said, "Maybe the diggings are way out somewhere. In that case they'd be self-contained."

"Maybe." Axilia wasn't convinced. "But there should be a feel to the place if there was. Miners like to spend their money and it shows. But this town is dead; no bars, casinos, girls—nothing. Maybe the Hausi knows. I'll ask him tomorrow."

"You want to work?" The woman serving the dinner had overheard. "Anna could use you. Or you could work the fishing boats. Are you a carpenter? A mason? Can you work in metal? Are you skilled in electronics?"

"I'm hungry." Axilia's face reflected his irritation. "Women," he grumbled as she moved away. "They never know when to mind their own business."

The meal was good; baked fish followed by slices of meat in a rich sauce and accompanied by a profusion of vegetables. A compote followed together with a cheese blended with syrup and laced with veins of emerald and cobalt. Anna had been generous with the wine.

Lifting his glass Ochen said, "A toast, my friends. To the best voyage we could have made!"

"The best?" Tocsaw shook his head. "The worst, maybe. I'll drink to that but not to the other."

"That's because you're a fool. Don't you know about Elysius? Man, it's ideal! You want something you just take it. You don't have to work. You just help yourself and no one will stop you."

Dumarest said, dryly, "I wouldn't like to try it."

"Why not? Scared?"

"You could say that."

"Of them?" Ochen gestured at the people standing at the bar, the others now sitting at small tables. "Sheep just waiting to be sheared. This is a soft world. I know. I met a man who'd lived here for years."

"If it was so good why did he leave?" Tocsaw helped himself to more wine. "Did he tell you that?"

"He did."

"You sleep on a hard floor all your life," said Quail, musingly. "When you do you long for a feather bed. Then you get one and, soon, you long for the hard floor again. It happens."

"A lot of things happen," said Axilia. "And the thing which happens most is meeting up with liars. That's what brought me to this damned world and I guess it brought you here too. The only difference is that you met up with a bigger liar than I did." He looked at Dumarest. "What about you, Earl? Were you the victim of a liar too?"

Perhaps, but if so the man would never lie again.

Zalman said, quickly, "Have none of you ever been to Elysius before? No? I thought not. If you had there would be no stupid talk of shearing sheep. Those who have goods know how to protect them and those who aren't interested in defending their property have nothing to steal. What you can do is work."

"You can do that anywhere." Quail refilled his glass with ruby wine. "That's not why I came to this world."

"So you want to sit and dream, is that it? Set yourself up with all the comforts and take it easy for the rest of your life." Zalman shrugged. "Well, why not? It's as good an ambition as any. How about you?" He looked at Ochen and Tocsaw. "The same. But not you, Sven, eh?"

"I came to find work. A man just can't sit and do nothing. Anyway, I need to build a stake. A big one." A hand rose to touch his ruined face. "What I need doesn't come cheap." Cosmetic surgery to make him whole again but the scar on his mind could never be healed. A memory which sent his hand to the decanter, to pour, to freeze as he set it down. "The bitch!" His tone rose with dazed incredulity. "The stinking bitch—here!"

She stood just within the open door, illuminated with dancing light from the swirling lanterns, swaths of color altering the hue of hair and eyes and giving her skin a luminous quality. A figure which a man dulled by drink

could take for another. One which could be taken for the
cause of pain and the target for revenge.

"Ieko!" The name was a shout as Axilia reared to his
feet, dishes rattling, a glass smashing as it hit the floor.
"Ieko—you whore!"

A name and insult which shocked the room to silence.
In the doorway the woman turned, frowning, to see the
scarred miner jump the table and come running toward
her, his glass in his hand. A glass which shattered as he
stooped to dash it against the floor, to become a ringed
ugliness of pointed shards which caught the light and
gleamed with the color of blood.

"At last!" His voice held gloating. "Remember when
last we met? The gift you gave me?" His head thrust
toward her in a snake-like gesture. "See? Note how pretty
it is. How well it would look on you." The glass rose,
threatening, turning in his hand. Multiple daggers to rip at
skin and flesh, to sever the nose, the lips, to blind the
eyes.

"No!" Zalman caught Dumarest's arm. "Earl, don't!"

A private quarrel and the extraction of revenge. The
woman could have earned it and the miner be in the right
according to his customs but Dumarest could not sit and
watch it done. Axilia, more drunk than he'd seemed, was
blood-crazed, an animal now bereft of all judgment. How
long ago had the woman thrown acid into his face? What
were the odds of them meeting again here?

"Ieko!" He had jumped between her and the door, bar-
ring her escape, and now stood, crouching, relishing his
moment. "Fate is good, you bitch! How often have I
prayed we should meet again? How many times have I
searched to find you? On Quand. On Helbrish. On a
dozen worlds where you could have been waiting. Now, at
last, we meet."

"No!" She backed, one hand lifted, eyes wide with terror. "You're mad! Mad!"

"Just as you made me, my dear." A step and the miner
was closer, the broken glass lifted, aimed, poised inches
from her eyes. "Pray, Ieko! Pray!"

The glass smashed in his hand, the plate Dumarest had

thrown spinning on to shatter as it glanced from a man standing at the bar. Axilia turned, snarling, the broken stem falling as he plunged a hand beneath his tunic. Steel shone as he drew a knife; ten inches of honed and pointed metal. A glow doubled as Dumarest lifted his own blade from his boot.

"Sven, you fool, listen to me!"

"Pimp! Stinking, dirty pimp! I'll see your guts, you bastard!"

A man crazed, lost in time, hate and anger boiling to give him a maniacal strength. His eyes were suffused with blood, froth edging the corners of his mouth, sweat dewing his skin. Already he was deaf and blind to reality, locked in a berserker frenzy. A machine, armed, primed to explode and Dumarest had made himself the target.

He backed, dodged, backed again and felt the impact of a table against his back. A barrier which held him as the blades touched, parted to touch again, filling the air with a thin, vicious ringing. Axilia was more dangerous than any opponent he had met in the arena; a man willing to expend his total energy in a wild burst of fury. Wounds wouldn't stop him. Cuts would be ignored. Only death could bring him down.

And he displayed an unexpected talent.

The table slid to one side as Dumarest threw his weight against it, toppled with a crash as he darted to one side, speed alone saving his face, the blinding slash aimed at his eyes whining through the air. An ordinary man would have been exposed then, thrown off balance by the force of his uninterrupted cut, but Axilia moved with it, using the momentum to spin and lower his arm to cut again.

Dumarest parried, moved back, weaved as he came forward, not wasting time on trying to delude the man or make cunning feints. It was enough for him, now, simply to survive.

"Scum!" Axilia had bitten his lip and blood masked mouth and chin. "Lousy pimp! Fight you stinking coward!"

Miner's talk and a change for the better. The initial fury was passing, vented on the air, and now he was slipping into a more cautious mold. For a time it would make him even more dangerous; a fighter's cunning added to the previous maniacal rage, and the knife he was using was evidence of experience. A ten-inch blade—the customary length for professionals.

It slashed, vanished to slash again, the blade turning so as to catch and reflect the light, turned again to lose its shine and become relatively invisible. A trick Dumarest had anticipated and his own blade, shorter by an inch, slammed hard against the other's wrist with numbing force. A blow with the flat aimed to disarm Axilia but failing in its intent. Slabbed muscle and tough sinew took and absorbed the blow, a boot rising in return to kick at a knee. Dumarest moved, felt the jar of it against his thigh and pressed forward to slam the weight of his clenched fist into the miner's face.

Blood from the broken nose mingled with that from the mouth.

"Bastard!" Axilia spat a carmine stream. "You dirty—"

The blades met as he attacked, the thin, spiteful ringing filling the chamber with the brittle music of combat. It merged with their panting, the scrape and thud of boots, the shift of bodies. Axilia was in trouble. The broken nose limited his breathing and the blood made gurgling noises as he sucked air. Also he was slowing, the insane pace he'd set impossible to maintain. As if realizing it he made a sudden, supreme effort.

"Earl!" Zalman was shouting. "Earl!"

Dumarest ignored the man. Axilia was close, teeth bared, stained with blood, more blood dappling his tunic. He flung out his left arm willing to take a cut in order to clear the path of his own attack. One which came in a splinter of light as he made the knife an extension of his arm, a claw ripping at Dumarest's throat.

He ducked, rose almost immediately, feeling the jar as the forearm hit his shoulder and then was in, aiming, striking, the pommel of his knife a hammer beating at the other's temple, the walls of his consciousness.

Axilia fell as though shot.

"Earl!" Zalman came running. "Are you hurt? There's blood on your face. A cut?"

"It's nothing." Dumarest looked at the fallen man. "Take care of him. Get the others to help. Wash his face and make sure he can breathe."

Only then did he look for the woman.

Chapter SIX

———◦◎◦———

He found her in the room outside, a small chamber fitted with soft furnishings and bathed with yellow light. A clear illumination which showed her as she really was. A woman in her fourth decade, the russet of her hair cut to form a helmet which framed a wide-boned face. The mouth was wide, the lips generous, the jaw round and determined. Her eyes, deep-set beneath winged brows, were blue, penetrating.

She said, "I am Isobel Boulaye. I thank you for saving my life."

"He didn't intend to kill you."

"But he did intend to maim." A hand rose to touch her cheek, the fingers drifting over the smoothly rounded skin. A gesture more revealing than she guessed; to some women the loss of beauty was more terrible than death. "But why? What reason could he have?"

"He thought you were someone else. A girl who had hurt him."

"I've never seen him before in my life."

"No." Dumarest wondered at her calm, knowing just how great the shock must have been, the fear. "The light confused him and he had been drinking."

As the woman had been. He watched as a girl refilled her glass and handed him another. Brandy. He took a sip and savored its warmth. The woman swallowed hers at a gulp.

"I needed that." She drew in her breath and he saw the stir and lift of her breasts beneath the shimmering fabric of her gown. Feminine attributes augmented by the nar-

61

row waist, the swell of hips and thighs. Her perfume was a spiced astringency. "Another?"

"I've enough." Dumarest took another sip. "A nasty experience, my lady, but, at least, you've suffered no lasting injury. Now if you will excuse me?"

"You're leaving?"

"I need to wash." The blood was drying on his face and the wound needed to be stanched. And he could use a shower.

She said, "Use my room. I can take care of the wound if you want, I've had some experience. Medicines too—please, you can't refuse!"

An obligation and one it would be kind to relieve her of. Also it was convenient. Dumarest nodded.

"Good!" Her pleasure was genuine. "I'll order some wine. It's room 9."

One smaller than that he shared with Zalman but with softer touches. The bed was wide, soft, bright with a woven cover. The window looked to the other side of the house and the carpet was soft beneath his feet. A bowl and faucet stood behind a painted screen.

Comfort—but the little signs were present in this room as the other. The hint of decay, the taint of neglect.

"Sit here, Earl." She smiled as he looked at her. "Yes, I know your name as I do the others. Anna gave them to me. I was coming to talk with you when that beast attacked. If you hadn't defended me—" She shuddered. "You could have killed him. You should have killed him—instead you told the others to take care of him. Why?"

"He was crazed, drunk, unknowing."

"Reasons for sparing his life? What if he comes after you seeking revenge?"

"He won't."

"But if he does you will kill him." She frowned, trying to understand. "Because then it would be a personal matter? Is that it? What he threatened to do to me wasn't really your concern and so you had no right to interfere. But you couldn't bear to see me hurt."

An explanation which seemed to satisfy her. He said, dryly, "No one else seemed interested in saving you."

"Those at the bar? The tables? No, why should they be." Wine had accompanied them and she poured and handed him a glass. "They are different. I—well, never mind. Your health, Earl, and my gratitude."

"And the use of your bowl?"

"Of course, you need to wash. Stay seated, I'll do it."

"No." It would be easier to do it himself. "With your permission?"

He stripped off his tunic without waiting for an answer and plunged his head into the filled bowl. The water stung, turned red, vanished as he pulled the plug and let it run down the drain. More followed, now a pale pink, and she handed him a towel when he rose, dripping.

"Now sit." Her tone brooked no argument. "Let me see that wound."

Her fingers were deft, probing, and he heard the hiss of indrawn breath as she parted his hair.

"Close, Earl. The scalp is slashed but if the cut had been deeper he could have exposed bone."

And deeper still the brain. Dumarest said, "Can you stanch it?"

"Easily. Just stay as you are."

He heard the rustle of her gown as she moved away, a click, the rustle again then a sharp sting which immediately faded.

"There! I've sealed it firm. In a few days the coating will vanish and you'll be as good as new." She hesitated, her tone changing, gaining added intensity. "Is there anything else I can do for you?"

"Please, some more wine?"

He watched as she poured, noting the flush now staining her cheeks, the elusive but unmistakable signals emitted by a woman yearning for a male. Signals which she needn't even be aware of but which he recognized as an animal could scent a spoor.

As she handed him the glass he said, "You were coming to talk to us. Why?"

"To offer you work. To ask you to help me. I've a

mine which—" She broke off as he smiled. "Something amuses you?"

"The man who attacked you is a miner. He's been looking for somewhere to work."

"He needn't waste his time!"

A natural reaction. Dumarest rose and crossed to the window. The days on Elysius were short and already it was dark. Even so it was early yet, few lights shone in the town. An oddity to add to others. Why had no one tried to help the woman? Why the neglect? What had made the Hausi mention colors in the sky? He could see none, merely traces of wispy cloud, a veil for the glow of blossoming starlight.

Where was the man Zalman had promised?

He said, "Were you born here?"

"No. My home world is Ascelius. I came here with my husband to work the mine. That was a long time ago it seems." She added, quickly, "He's dead now. Dead and buried."

An explanation for her need. Dumarest caught the odor of her perfume as she came closer, the nearing heat of her body against his naked torso. He turned to face her, feeling the touch of her fingers as they traced the line of scars marking his chest.

"A fighter," she mused. "I should have guessed it. No one else could have fought as well." Her hands lingered as they moved over his ribs, the sharply defined muscles, moving toward his back as if with a life of their own.

"Earl!"

"You know the people here?" He made no attempt to step away. "You could tell me about them?"

"People!" She drew in her breath and then, abruptly, dropped her hands and stepped to where she had placed the wine. He watched the pulse of her throat as she drank. "I suppose I know them. Who are you looking for? A girl? Someone young and lovely?"

"A man. Probably old. Possibly a scholar of some kind. One who could be fond of books and antiquities." He sensed her surprise. "I doubt if he's a native but he could be. A man who could live alone and is probably laughed at. Someone who believes in the truth of legends."

She said nothing, pouring wine, drinking to pour again. A woman gaining time or one striving to achieve emotional control? Zalman could have read her but he could only guess.

Dumarest urged, "Please—to me it is important. It's possible you know of such a person."

"His name?"

"I don't know it." A secret Zalman retained. "I don't know where he lives." Another. "Nor what he looks like." A situation he'd had to accept but which must shortly change.

He looked at the glass she handed to him, the wine it contained. She said, "A toast, Earl—to lost causes! I'm sorry, but I can't help you. I know of none who would fit your description." As if sensing his disbelief she added, "I live in an isolated house and work an isolated mine. I have no visitors, no friends, few acquaintances. The only times I come to town are to collect supplies, deliver a shipment, and to try to gain labor from any new arrivals. I don't socialize. I've no interest in anyone on this damned world and no one has any interest in me. No one!"

Dumarest heard the words and caught the pain they contained, the bleak, aching loneliness. He remained silent, the tension in the room was as brittle as the glass in his hand. The glass she held which shattered as she let it fall to come toward him, to hold him, to offer herself in abject surrender.

"Earl! For God's sake—Earl!"

It was dawn when he woke and he lay looking at the pattern of light thrown in pale colors on the ceiling from the uncurtained window. Beside him Isobel lay like a relaxed child, her face smoothed, eased of tensions, young again and revealing the beauty she had been so terrified to lose. A woman who had found a sudden happiness and who had grasped at it without question as to its possible duration. One who had reacted to the pressure of her need.

One he had shared, responding to it, engulfed by it, tensions induced by combat and fear exploding in a mutual release.

"Earl?" She moved, one hand questing, coming to rest as it touched his shoulder. "I love you, my darling. I love you."

Words born of a need, released by his proximity, her reaction to his maleness. A woman who had been alone too long. Gently he moved her hand and slipped from the bed. To wake her would be to add to the pain of parting. Later, if they met, she would have only pleasant memories.

The house was silent as he closed the door. A narrow passage led to the room he shared with Zalman and he moved quietly along it. Axilia had been put in a cubicle next door and he stepped into it to look at the man on the bed. He was asleep, his temple bearing an ugly bruise, his nose swollen, puffed over the thin tubes inserted into his nostrils. Dumarest checked them and the bone beneath the bruise. If it was cracked that was the worst. The man would live to work and fight another day.

In their own room Zalman was asleep.

He lay on one side, one hand close to his mouth, his breath disturbing the fine hairs on the backs of the fingers and palm. His clothing lay beside him and Dumarest reached toward it, freezing as the man stirred.

"Wha. . .?" Zalman moved, eyes closed, a man moving in his sleep but his hand darted like a snake up and beneath his pillow. Dumarest clamped it in his fingers, feeling the flesh, the bone, the metal of a laser. It was small, expensive, deadly at short range. "Earl!" Zalman ceased to struggle. "What the hell are you playing at?"

"Read me!"

"Don't play games. What time is it?" He blinked at the glowing windows fighting to free his hand. "All right if that's the way you want it. You grabbed me because you wanted to be sure I didn't shoot you by mistake. That I'd take you for an intruder. Well, I'm awake now and you can let me go."

He sat upright, scowling, rubbing at the welts on his hand. Dumarest watched his eyes, their flicker toward the untouched clothing. They could be innocent but the boots could have hollow heels, the tunic hold documents in the lining.

"Hans, it's time we had a talk."

"Later. I've a headache. We got to drinking after you'd gone and I've a devil with a hammer hard at work in my skull." Zalman's eyes were bloodshot and he looked as if he told the truth. "You had a better night than I did."

"Maybe."

"No doubt about it. Incidentally, I checked Axilia's pockets. He's got just about enough to pay his way for three days. After that he's stranded."

Information he could have done without, what had made Zalman mention it? Dumarest said, "When will you be ready to talk?"

"About what? Of course, the man we came to find. Earl, I have yet to discover where he might be. Give me time and all will be arranged."

"His name?"

Zalman shook his head. "I trust you, Earl, but old habits are hard to discard. I must keep something in reserve. Once you have found the man I will have completed my share of our bargain, but, if you find him without my assistance, what then?" He yawned, not waiting for an answer or perhaps he had read it. "Please, Earl, could you do me a service? Ask them downstairs to send up some hot tisane and tablets to ease my head."

Early as it was Anna was awake and busy. Dumarest found her in the kitchen, arms bare, sweat dewing her broad face. She was kneading dough and he watched as she made various shapes; snakes, fish, animals, and flowers.

"Rolls," she explained. "It's all bread but it adds variety. I bake a lot then freeze what we don't use for later." She frowned when Dumarest told her his errand. "His head? I wouldn't have thought so—he went easy on the wine. Maybe it was something he ate? Some people can't tolerate certain spices. Well, never mind, we'll soon have him fit."

A pot of stew stood on a stove and Dumarest tasted it as a young lad, little more than a child, went to tend Zalman. There were other youngsters in the kitchen, he noticed, girls budding into womanhood, boys approaching manhood.

"They like it in here," she said when he asked about them. "The workers like to know their kids are safe and the rest don't care what happens to them. I just feed them and they help out in return. Not that there's much they can do but every little helps."

"Has it always been like this?"

"Like what? Places run down, labor short, repairs needing to be done? I guess you must have noticed. I don't know." She added, slapping at the dough, "It could have been different and I guess it must have been but that was before my time. I wasn't born here, you understand. I came with my parents oh, a long time ago. We stayed with the owner of this place and when he died I took over."

"And your parents?"

"Forget them—I have."

A point he didn't press. A bowl stood on the table and he filled it with the stew at her invitation, sitting to spoon the succulent food into his mouth. Eating he looked around. The place was clean, well-fitted, filled with enticing smells; freshly baked bread, spices, fruits and nuts and pungent tisanes.

"That man you fought," she said, abruptly "Axilia?"

"Sven Axilia. What about him?"

"Has he money?"

"Some." She had been more than generous. "Enough to pay his keep until he is fit to move. A couple of days, say."

"As I thought. And then?" At his silence she added, "Is he willing to work?"

Would he have a choice? Dumarest said, "He'll work. Are you thinking of employing him?"

She misunderstood his tone. "He's ugly, I know, but he can't help that. And he lost his temper but maybe he had reason. Yes, I can use him. He's strong if nothing else."

And the roof wanted fixing and the plumbing and there would be stone to haul and stores to shift. Boxes and crates and bales too heavy for children to handle. Skills needed which they didn't possess.

Dumarest set down the empty bowl. As he stood Celia entered the kitchen to stand before the floured table.

"She's awake, mother."

"And thirsty?"

"Yes, she wants—"

"I know what she wants." Anna wiped her hands and moved to a cupboard from which she took a flask, a box and a tall glass. The flask held an amber liquid which she poured into the glass. "Here!" She held out some on a spoon for Dumarest to taste. "Recognize it?"

It was sweet, heavy with glucose, laced with vitamins, thick with protein. The basic which was the food of spacemen, one cup providing energy enough for a day.

"Is she hungry?"

"Estelle? She needs feeding up but it's more than that." From the box Anna took a heaped measure of a glittering powder and added it to the liquid in the glass. It flashed, twinkling, vanishing as it blended with the fluid. She offered none for Dumarest to taste.

"What's that?"

"Manna." She sounded defiant. "She needs it if anyone does and her sister knows she's getting it. Mtouba contacted her and she phoned me. She'll be coming to collect Estelle sometime this morning. I guess you'll be glad to see her go."

When she left he would go with her—the gratitude of her family was his only resource.

The screen died and Elge leaned back in his chair palming his eyes. Against the darkness retinal images danced, blurred with fatigue. Elysius—a word with multiple applications. Was it a flower, a drug, a drink, a dance, a mixture, a manner of speech, a method of prayer, of meditation, of exercise? The list seemed endless; meanings garnered and fed into computers to be assessed and related to orders of probability.

Many had already been eliminated. To search for the origin of the word if it had been a personal name was to waste time. The field of art held little hope—cybers would not be influenced by such an emotion-laden area. Foods—who could tell what a man assimilated during his lifetime? Flowers? Systems? Attitudes? All possible but of a very low order of probability. A drug? More promising but analysis had revealed no sign of any foreign compound down to molecular level. Virus infection, radioactive poisoning, radiation—all had been eliminated.

Yet the word remained.

Opening his eyes Elge reached for his communicator panel.

"Master?"

"Has a check been made on all movements and associations of both affected units?"

The answer was immediate. "Check made and result negative. No connection with anything appertaining to elysius."

As expected and had anything been discovered he would have been notified as a matter of urgent priority. The act of asking, in itself, was betraying proof of the accumulated toxins of fatigue now dulling his intelligence. Soon, in order to maintain his efficiency, he must sleep but before then time remained in which to work.

A touch and again the screen flared to life. It was not necessary for a cyber to clutter his mind with facts; data was more efficiently stored in electronic memories, but it was essential for him to know what to look for and determine its value. Association was the key to successful prediction; to be aware of relationships no matter how subtle, to build from them a platform from which to extrapolate the whole.

Elysius—there had to be a significance.

Words flowed on the screen, halted as he read the glowing letters, moved on to halt again as he pressed buttons and dictated references. Often the answer could be

found in the beginnings; a clue so obvious as to be over-
looked.

ELYSIUS—a word most probably derived from Elysian.

ELYSIAN—a word derived from Elysium.

ELYSIUM—a place of future happiness.

The answer?

In his expansion through the galaxy man had carried
with him many old items of furniture; names which now
identified many worlds. Eden, Holme, Heevan, Padrise,
Nirvana, Olipius—a list of distortions, names shortened,
changed, altered with the erosion of time and usage. Elysium—Elysian—Elysius—the connection was obvious.

A world?

But, if so, which?

The screen flared again, settled to relay the information. There were seven which could be the one all, at one
time, promising settlers to be a place of future happiness.
Was it the one close to a red giant? A world of steaming
seas and torrid forests? That, to colonists from an ice-
bound planet, would have seemed desirable. The one illuminated by triple suns giving constant daylight? To
people from a nighted sphere it would have held merit.
The one with rolling meadows and running streams? The
one with mighty glaciers?

Again he called the technicians.

"Run a check on all possible errors in the pronuncia-
tion of the word 'elysius' in the recordings. Look for any
distortions and test aligned harmonics to isolate and plot
any deviation. Also make a check on all variables."

"All, master?"

"All."

The word had seven letters which meant more than five
thousand combinations to be checked for any association.
Bad enough, but any distortion in the recording itself
could widen the range and increase the load. A task impossible without the aid of machines—but one which had
to be done.

Chapter SEVEN

The House of Lamont was long, low, built of stone cut and set in pleasing designs. The sharply pointed roof had upswept eaves, the windows mullioned, graced with pointed arches. An inner courtyard held a pool and a fountain shaped in the aspect of intertwined figures. A surrounding gallery was supported on columns carved with elaborate convolutions. The wide gates were of metal set with suspended gongs.

A big, rambling house with lichen on the tiles and vegetation clinging to the walls; vines and creepers dotted with delicate blooms. One with estates and farms and the sea providing a susurrating music from the shore below the nearby cliffs. A castle with an absent king.

"Have patience, Earl." Selina Lamont came up from behind him and dropped her hand on his arm. "There's no hurry. Jarvis will be back soon."

Her uncle, the head of the family, as she was Estelle's elder sister. Dumarest turned to look into the clear pools of her eyes. Dark, almost black, as was her hair, the long lashes which rested like moths on her cheeks when she closed her eyes. Her skin held a summer's warmth and her body, slim, lithe, held the peculiar disjointedness of a born athlete.

"Let's run," she urged. "Or swim. Or join the others in a picnic." Her smile faded as he shook his head. "No? Why not, Earl? What's the point in standing on this balcony looking at the sky? Jarvis will arrive when he gets here and nothing will bring him sooner."

"You sent him word?"

"Of course, but he knows that Estelle is in good hands and having the best of care."

Treatment which had worked a miraculous change. Dumarest looked at her where she sported with others beyond the open gate. The vacuousness had gone, the emptiness, the taint of the peculiar blight. Now she was happy, laughing as she caught and threw a ball, vibrant with health. A girl who'd suffered an unpleasant dream but was now awake.

A change which had been apparent when they had left the tavern and which seemed now, after three days, complete.

Three days?

Had it been as long as that?

Dumarest felt the prickle of impatience but there was nothing he could do. Selina had greeted him, made him welcome, flown him back to the house in a raft which had been slow and unwieldy. A craft which had gone on to pick up her uncle.

Three days?

His room was comfortable, the bed soft, the food and wine excellent. Things to match the company and it had been good to rest and let the hours slip past. Selina had made them enjoyable as had the others and there had been walks and sports and contests of skill and strength and, it seemed, endless laughter. A party which promised never to cease.

"Come on, Earl, let's swim." Selina, impatient, made her decision. "I'll meet you on the beach."

She was gone, running like a sprite, thin fabric hugging the contours of her body. An unspoiled child of nature who had come to him in the night.

Had it been the first night? The second?

She had drifted into his room like a ghost, slipping into bed beside him, naked, her body cool as were the hands which had caressed him. A creature of softness eager to play an ancient game and, for her, it had been nothing more. A shallow appeasing of the senses; touches and kisses and movements leading to a desired culmination.

At the end she had smiled and stretched and ran her fingers through his hair as if a child pleased with a new toy.

Now, as he watched, she turned and waved and ran on toward the sea.

Again Dumarest searched the sky.

It was as empty as before; thin wisps of cloud far over the ocean, pale smudges of color a thin smoke over the hills. The wind was gentle and the sea, where he could see it in the distance, calm.

Why was Jarvis taking so long?

A man, the head of his family, would surely be concerned over Estelle's welfare? Eager to learn how she had been found and eager too, Dumarest hoped, to recompense the one who had found her. A reward would be normal. The information he could give would be, possibly, of higher value.

"Earl!" Selina, back, was calling to him. "Come on, Earl! Hurry!"

He wore nothing but shorts; the gray of his tunic, pants and boots a somber blotch on the bright carpet of his room, but more was unnecessary and he headed toward the stairs and ran barefoot over the sward beyond the gate. Selina was waiting for him, breaking into a run as he appeared, long legs flashing, little plumes of sand spurting from beneath her feet as she reached the wide, sandy beach.

Others were present, some young, more nearing middle age, a few old and strolling but all paid attention to the race.

"Selina!" shouted a youth. "I'll back you! Win and I'll take a chore!"

"I back Earl," screamed a girl. "Two tasks if you lose, Selina!"

Bets which were lost in the wind as Dumarest raced over the sand, feeling the heightening exhilaration of his blood, the lifting euphoria. The world narrowed to the racing figure of the girl, the need to exist only to catch her, to pass her and to win the race. A need which closed the gap between them, which brought her level, which sent him ahead to plunge into the ocean.

"Bravo!" The girl who had backed him stood clapping her hands. "You take two of my tasks, Selina."

"And one from me!" shouted the youth. "You lost and owe me a chore."

Laughing Selina said, "Double or quits? Let's race to the float!"

It rested a quarter of a mile out to sea, moored by ropes, splotched with patches of color. Immediately the water was filled with splashing figures as a crowd of others followed the girl toward it. Watching, Dumarest knew she would win.

The plunge had cooled him a little and checked the mounting intoxication. One he thought about as he returned to the beach. It had been a moment of near-hysteria in which all caution had threatened to be lost. To race over a strange shore, to plunge into unknown waters—what if there had been rocks?

There hadn't been so why worry about it?

Why worry about anything?

It was better to lie back on the yielding sand and study the enigmatic shapes made by the drifting clouds in the azure dome of the sky; wisps which made men and beasts and cities of smoke and imagination. To let the mind wander and probe into interesting regions of speculation; would Selina come to him again tonight? Should he go to her? To one of the others—the girl who had backed him could be interesting. To take a long walk toward the hills? To swim? To play with what fish might be lurking beneath the water?

Or just to lie and look at the sky and the dot growing bigger as it came toward him. The raft which dropped down toward the house to land.

Jarvis Lamont was old, withered, looking like a gnome as he sat in his chair. A cap of scarlet fabric covered his balding skull and a robe of vermilion and green hid his frail body but there was nothing frail or colorful about his eyes. They were as pale as the sky and as hard as diamond.

"You returned Estelle to us," he said abruptly. "And you will be expecting a reward."

"Recompense." Dumarest looked across the wide desk behind which the man sat. "Has she told you the story?"

"I have seen her." A thin hand lifted, waved, "She was vague."

"With reason."

"Possibly. Do you wish to relate it?"

"No." Why was the man arguing? Dumarest said, "There is nothing I can tell you she couldn't do as well. Perhaps she prefers to forget the entire incident."

As he wanted to get the present one over. The raft had broken his introspection and Jarvis had been impatient. Surely he could have waited until dusk? And now the questioning. What point did it have? Estelle had been returned and it was a matter of family honor to settle any expenses incurred.

"Recompense," mused the old man. "Just what is the sum in question?" He blinked at the answer. "So much?"

"There was her passage to be refunded together with a sum for her purchase. Also her lodging at the tavern. And there is a matter of personal inconvenience." Why didn't the man just settle the debt? Dumarest ended, "If you are pleased to have her back surely you will not begrudge the money?"

"Begrudge it? No. Being able to find it is another matter." A flask of wine stood on the desk before him, green, lustrous with shimmering particles, and before Dumarest could comment Jarvis gestured toward it. "You must be thirsty, Earl. Help yourself to wine."

Thirsty? Dumarest was suddenly conscious of the dryness of his mouth. He poured, looked at his host, set aside the flask at the other's negative gesture.

"Drink, Earl. I am old and wine does not agree with me, but go ahead." He nodded as Dumarest swallowed. "You have been here how long? Four days? Three?"

"In your house? Four days tomorrow."

"On Elysius?"

"Add a day."

"Finish your wine, my friend. Almost five days—long

enough for you, surely, to have noticed certain things. The courtyard, for example? The condition of the rooms? The house itself—need I go on?"

A courtyard with cracked and broken flags, the pool empty, the fountain dry. Rooms with a bucket instead of running water. Bathrooms which held dust and accumulated debris. The house itself which repeated the pattern he'd noticed in town. A pattern he recognized.

Dumarest said, "Money—you've got no money."

"That is correct."

"But you have estates, fields—"

"Wealth isn't fruit you pluck from a tree, my friend." The old, thin voice was bitter. "It comes from profit and that is wrung from the sweat of labor. And, if you have no labor?"

"You've people." Dumarest looked at his glass, the dregs of emerald wine. "Young men and women."

"None of whom are willing to work. Some small tasks they cannot avoid but even those they try to pass on. You wondered what took me so long to get here? To greet my niece? Perhaps you thought I didn't care." Jarvis looked at the hand lying before him on the desk, the thin fingers clenched to show the strained skin, the gleam of bone. "My own sister's child," he said quietly. "An orphan now that her mother is dead. Would you believe that she has never asked after her? After the mother who bore her— the woman she helped to kill!"

Dumarest said nothing, waiting.

"We searched," said Jarvis after a moment. "I looked until I could look no more and Marie drove herself too far beyond the edge of exhaustion. The word came later—she had been seen on the field just before a ship left for Cenalas. Mervin was dead and I was too old to travel and who else was willing? So there was nothing to do but wait."

Wait and pray and hope against hope that, one day, word would come that she was alive and well and if nothing else that would have been enough. Dumarest looked again at his glass, thinking of the unthinking cruelty of youth. Was cruelty born of ignorance worse than that created by disregard? What had made the girl run?

A question he asked as he helped himself to more wine.

"Nothing." Jarvis spread his hands as he recognized the stupidity of the answer. "That is nothing external—she was not beaten or bullied or denied in any way. I doubt if she even ran as you are using the word. She just left when the chance presented itself. A mood. A momentary whim—God, man, can't you understand?"

A step into an enticing parlor there to be caught by the web of circumstance. A journey to be paid for and, after the landing, food and shelter to be gained. A young and nubile girl lacking any practical skill and experience—helpless prey for waiting harpies.

Dumarest said, "The purchase price I mentioned was to free her from her labor contract; she had been indentured to a governess to help in a managerial household. The woman who accompanied her told me she'd been working in a hospital after being admitted for therapeutic care. They indentured her to offset accumulated medical debts over and above those cancelled by her labor."

A lie which Jarvis wanted to hear. He said, "I owe you much, Earl. No—you've had enough of that wine. Here, try some of this and I will join you." He produced a bottle, sealed, containing a clear amber fluid. "Your health!"

After the other it was tart, stimulating.

Dumarest said, "You were born on this world?"

"Yes." Jarvis blinked as Dumarest asked the questions he had put to Isobel. "A scholar? Someone interested in antiquities and legends? No, Earl, I know no one of such a nature, but that means nothing. I rarely leave the house and was away when you arrived only to arrange for workers to tend the harvest. Fruit," he explained. "A cross from mutated hybrids. My father put them in when a young man and each day I thank him for his foresight. It could be the last trip I shall make."

"You give up too easily," smiled Dumarest. "You're not that old."

"Perhaps, but age is not the only reason. The raft flew erratically as you may have noticed. The driver is working on it but repairs take time and may be impossible. In the meantime you are my guest." Jarvis sipped at his wine. "Earl, about your expenses. I can offer you a home for as long as you want it. A share in all we have. All the comforts to be gained." His tone revealed he knew of Selina's activities. "But I can't give you money. It would give me comfort to know that you understand."

An old man clinging to his pride, watching the slow decline of his house, his family. Dumarest said, "I understand. Just arrange for me to get back to town."

As a driver the man was bad, as an engineer he was hopeless. Dumarest looked at the raft, the covers removed from the engine and left to one side. The power unit itself hadn't been touched. How long had it been? Three days? Four?

He frowned, trying to remember, but the need for urgency escaped him. A day, two days, what did it matter? But the mess annoyed him; no machinery should be left that way. On impulse he went in search of the mechanic. He was lying beneath a flowering bush, a girl beside him, another feeding him wine.

He blinked as Dumarest loomed above him.

"Earl! You want something?"

"You said the raft would be ready today."

"Did I?" Boyce shook his head. "I'll get around to it later."

"When?"

"Later." He ran a hand over the thigh of the girl at his side. "There's no hurry."

A sentiment echoed by Selina when, later, they rested in relaxed abandon on his bed.

"You don't have to leave, Earl. I don't want you to leave." She smiled and snuggled close. "Let the raft wait."

As Zalman could wait. Zalman! Dumarest had forgotten the man but what did it matter? Even so the condition of the raft had annoyed him. Mtouba could be contacted and a vehicle sent out but that would mean expense and that was something he couldn't afford. The raft—it had to be the raft.

"Tomorrow," murmured the girl when he said so. "You can look at it tomorrow."

"Me?"

"Boyce, then, if he gets around to it. Earl, come closer. Closer." She sighed as she pressed herself against him. "That's better. Why worry about that old raft when there are so much nicer things to do?" Her lips were moist against his own. "Like that." Her hands moved. "And like this." Flesh slid smoothly over his own. "And like this, darling. We'll fly later."

He said, remembering, "When there is color?"

"What?"

"Something the Hausi said about there being color in the sky. Maybe we could see it."

"Fly into it, you mean?" She reared from where she lay against him, eyes sparkling with excitement. "Earl, that's wonderful! I've never done that. We'll do it together. We'll go up and up and right into the colors and—when, my darling? When?"

"As soon as the raft is ready. You'll help me?"

"Yes! Yes! I'll offer to do all his chores if he gets it ready in time. How long do we have? Two days?" She frowned, then her face cleared. "It doesn't matter. But you'll take me with you, Earl? You promise?"

She was a child begging a treat, smiling even wider as he nodded, bending forward to kiss him, to hide his face in the thick, dark veil of her hair. And then, all at once, she wasn't a child any longer but a grown and demanding woman.

"Earl!"

A thing of softness and warmth as Isobel had been— why did he think of her? She had been driven by inner hurt and aching loneliness, emotions using her body to gain relief, those same emotions converting a simple act of copulation into something verging on the mystical. An ecstasy so intense it had become a thing apart; the act itself an accompaniment rather than the nexus.

"Earl!" Selina was demanding. "Earl—please!"

He rose, pushing her from him, rising to cross the room and stare through the window at the night beyond. Had she regretted it? Did she now feel cheapened, ashamed? Had he been kind in leaving her as he had? Did he care?

The night held smells; the odor of growing things, perfume from the flowers, the brine scent from the sea. Above blazed a host of stars and, even as he watched, a trail of fire crossed the heavens. A meteor—but it could have been a ship. How long had he stayed here? What had happened to the hours? The days? Why did he still remain?

He heard a rustle from behind him and a liquid gurgling. Selina came to stand beside him, glasses in her hand. She handed him one and he saw the glint of sparkles swirling in the liquid, tiny gems illuminated by starlight.

"Tomorrow," she whispered. "Worry about it tomorrow."

A new day and a new resolve. The raft to be repaired and a promise to be kept. Tomorrow—or the day after—the wine coated his mouth with sweetness.

And, after the wine, came her kisses.

Chapter EIGHT

At first there had been hope, then hurt, now there was only a dull resignation. She had loved and lost—would it have been better not to have loved at all? To have loved in a way unknown with Rudi who had always treated her as if she had been made of fragile glass. And Dumarest had surprised her. A hard, ruthless man. A trained fighter, a killer, a barbarian according to her previous standards, one whom she would have sworn would be rough and selfish, uncaring for anything other than the satisfying of his need. Yet there had been none of the assumed brutality. Instead there had been gentleness and consideration—the man had cared.

Memory created a resurgence of desire and again she felt the touch of his skin, smelt the odor of him; the reek of a man who had fought and shed blood—a warrior male exuding basic pheromones to which she had responded. He had fought for her—how could she have denied him the fruits of victory?

A justification and one which sent her from the bed to stand beneath the thrusting stream of the shower. A hot stream; at least the solar unit was still in working order, and she reveled in it, turning to feel its impact on breasts and buttocks, on belly and back. How could she have been so weak?

Rudi would have had the answer and she could imagine him delivering it had he been alive and she confessing.

"Abstinence, my dear, a simple matter of basic hunger. A starving man will eat and pay no attention to the qual-

ity of the food. You were hungry and needed to be fed.
Don't worry about it."

Don't worry, but Rudi was dead and buried in the hills
and Dumarest had ignored her.

The shower died and she, dried, returned to the bedroom. Gisel was back; a cup of tisane stood beside the
bed, late but still welcome. The cook had also returned
and so, no doubt, had Chell. She was not surprised; the
house offered shelter, warmth, food, and protection.
While she was fool enough to tolerate them they would
remain even though it was on their terms.

"Your favorite, madam." The cook set down a plate as
she sat at the table. "I cooked it just as I know you like
it."

Her memory was bad; she had cooked what Rudi had
liked and had done it badly. Isobel poked at the food,
forcing herself to eat a little, knowing she needed the
strength. And yet what good would it be? A negative attitude about which she needed no warning, but one hard to
change.

Down below Chell was sitting with his back against the
wall staring at the raft. He looked at her as she entered
the storeroom, making no attempt to rise. His smile was
empty, inane.

"Get on your feet!" He blinked as she snapped the order, but reluctantly obeyed. "This raft should be loaded
by now. Why isn't it?"

"Did you want it to be?" He smiled again. "I'll see to
it."

"When—next year?" Sarcasm was wasted; it simply
didn't register. "Never mind. Get it done immediately.
Understand?" His casual disregard infuriated her. "Listen,
you! While you use my house and eat my food you do
what I tell you—is that clear? Load that raft. If it isn't
ready by the time I return I never want to see you again!"

A warning which he would forget as soon as she left
the room; one he probably hadn't even heard, but, at
times, it was impossible for her to remain silent. At least
she needn't watch and she climbed the stairs, almost running up the last few steps leading to the roof.

The sky over the hills was, thank God, empty of devils but even as she watched a plume of color rose to the north; a twisting column of indigo which shredded to take the form of a cavorting satyr before becoming a somber mist against the bright azure. Another joined it, this time a vivid chrome, yellow merging with the blue to form a writhing combination of greens at the edges; a veil to shroud a lined and brooding face.

For a moment the image held her so that she stood careless of the wind which ruffled the helmet of her hair, feeling her stomach constrict at the visage, the empty sockets of the eyes, the gap which formed the mouth. Rudi? Could he be restless in his sleep and now be watching her with silent accusation?

A fantasy and one which dissolved as the face, torn by the wind, altered to form another shape which in turn joined with the indigo in spreading dissolution. Rudi was fast in the Fulden Hills while the image she had seen was to the north—yet did ghosts recognize the limitations of distance?

And what reason could he have for accusation?

She saw his face again against the closed lids of her eyes, the look, the horror, the knowledge frozen in the moment of death now stamped indelibly on her memory. A man knowing he was to die, feeling the pain, the shock of impending extinction.

God—why had it happened?

If she had forced him to stay with her for those few minutes longer—demanded his help in some small way, or if she had acted faster, joined him, been with him—need it have happened?

Guilt, she thought. Yet why should she feel guilty? Of all men Rudi would have understood and, understanding, forgive. A matter of a simple, biological hunger, a basic need—yes, he would have understood. Then why did she feel as she did? Why was she hugging the memory of Dumarest as a sword to stab her heart?

Why was he ignoring her?

The reason, she knew, for her inner restlessness. The root of the need to justify and explain. There was no guilt, no need for confession, no cause to seek a dead man's absolution. She was thinking as a child, trying to shed responsibility, unwilling to accept the truth. Dumarest owed her nothing; already he had been more than kind.

Another gust of color reared toward the sky, a twisting column of orange which painted a broad smear across the heavens, one which fanned to the impact of the wind, writhing to form an expanse of brilliant filigree. Against it, for the first time, she saw the raft.

Selina was euphoric, radiating a burning pleasure, skin, hair, her entire body betraying an inner joy. "Look!" The lift of her hand pointed to the widening expanse of orange. "It's beautiful! And there, Earl, see?"

A mound swelling beneath the sun, small from their present height, a point of taut membrane among the ochre rocks which studded the ground below. More ephemerae ripening to embark on the final stage of their life-cycle— Dumarest had learned the meaning of the colors which smeared the sky. Another lay a short distance from it, still more farther toward the loom of the hills.

"I've never done this before." Selina leaned against him, softly warm, the scent of her hair a natural perfume. "Jarvis would never let us use the raft and the wind from the sea keeps the color blowing inland. He couldn't have known what it was like. Earl, it's fantastic! It's just like riding on the back of a bird."

One crippled, old, slow to respond. Boyce had sworn the raft was as good as it would ever be and had proved it by taking the controls but, from the first, it had been erratic, veering when there was no wind, dropping when the air was steady. A bad driver or fading plates? An engine which could no longer feed a steady flow of power to the antigrav units or an unnecessary anxiety? Dumarest had shared the other's careless acceptance at first but, as they rose to fly over broken ground and rocky soil the wind had cleared his head a little.

He said, "Maybe we should land."

"No!"

"We can go ahead on foot." A suggestion which he recognized as foolish even as he made it. The ground was too rough, such progress would take too long. "Or try again later." He gripped the edge of the raft as it tilted. "Boyce! Watch what you're doing!"

"It's all right." The driver turned, smiling. "Why worry, Earl? Just hang on and enjoy the ride."

"Hold on to me and enjoy life," whispered Selina. "Earl, darling, it would be wonderful to make love like this. To ride high above the ground and under the stars and for you to hold me and take me until the dawn came to show us where we were. Shall we do it, darling? Tonight?"

"Maybe."

"I mean it, Earl." She wriggled to face him. "Just you and me together. Can you fly a raft? Can you?" She relaxed as he nodded. "Tonight, then. Or we can land and leave Boyce and do it now. Among the colors, Earl. That would be wonderful!"

A novelty which she was eager to enjoy. Dumarest shook his head, aware of a dullness, a lack of concentration. Was the raft flying as it should or was it the man at the controls? The horizon was shifting before his eyes, veering, tilting, vanishing as the prow rose to appear again as it fell. An effect which could have been caused by badly loaded cargo, but the vehicle held only themselves and the driver.

"Earl?"

"A moment." He moved from the girl and examined the body of the machine. It was a normal craft, one used extensively by farmers, the body fifteen feet long, five wide, the rail as high above the ground when landed. A bench ran down both sides and the driver sat at the controls facing the front. If there had ever been a protective canopy it had been removed. The paint was scratched and in spots bare metal shone; twin signs of age and neglect. Beneath the covers, as he had seen, the connections were patched, twisted when they should have been soldered, screwed when they should have been welded. "Boyce, how's the lift?"

"You want to ride higher?" The man shrugged. "Then higher we go."

In turbulent air it was safer to ride high; the greater distance from the ground lessened the effect of rising thermals as well as providing more scope to regain control should the raft hit pockets of less density. But Dumarest hadn't wanted to rise higher but to check on the mechanical efficiency of the vehicle.

It rose slowly, more slowly than when they had left the house, tilting as Boyce manipulated the controls.

"The trim's not what it should be," he said casually. "But it's nothing to worry about."

Maybe, and he could be right, the emergency power should enable them to land should the main plant go. But if the raft should tilt too far there was a danger of being thrown out.

"Earl?" Selina moved away as he tried to lash her fast with the straps running along the bench. "What are you doing?"

"Just making sure you're safe."

"By tying me to the rail? No, Earl, I won't let you do it. I want to be free to move if I want." She rose, hands lifting, weaving to illustrate. "To sing and dance. Will you dance with me, darling? Hold me close and force me to move to your rhythm? The wind will be our music, Earl. Listen to it. Listen!"

Pay attention to the gusts, the sudden flurries which came like padded hammers to stir hair and sting the eyes. The blasts which attacked the raft as if it were an enemy to be replaced by soothing breezes droning a lullaby.

Hot air, rising, caught and diverted by the hills, merging with that from the sea, the draught from the natural funnel of the valley. It was no mystery why the colors swirled in such elaborate confusion.

"Down!" Dumarest sensed the danger. "Damn you, man, get us down!"

"Why? Because of a little wind? Hell, man, this is fun."

"Do it!" Dumarest spun as Selina caught at his arm. "Order him down, girl. Down!"

She laughed in his face. "Stop worrying, Earl." Her arm lifted, long fingers pointing. "See?"

Amber spurted from a ruptured sac, rising to form an obscene shape in the sky, changing to depict a mansion, an octopus, a cowled and enigmatic figure. Lavender joined it followed by a stream of puce. Looking over the edge of the raft Dumarest saw the ground below dotted with taut membranes.

"Away, Boyce! Away!"

He was too late. Even as he shouted the order the membrane below split with the report of a gun and, suddenly, they were enveloped in an olive darkness. One which was alive. One which could kill.

"Earl!"

Selina screamed as the ephemerae enveloped her, covering her face, her eyes, resting thickly on her hair, replaced by others as she swept them away with her hands. Winged bodies inches long, goggle-eyed, spined, spindle-legged, churning, swirling, locked in the mating frenzy. Individually they were harmless but as a mass they blinded, hampered, blocked the passage of air to the lungs, stopped ears, filled nostrils.

And the weight of them threatened the stability of the raft.

Dumarest felt it tilt as he grabbed at the girl, one hand gripping her wrist while the other kept his eyes clear of the swarm. Boyce was shouting, arms lifted, waving, a darker patch in the living darkness. One which slipped and fell against the controls.

Dumarest grabbed at the rail as the raft fell from beneath him, hanging, supported by one hand, the other clamped on Selina who dangled beneath him. A tearing weight which threatened his grip as the ephemerae closed in a ball about his head. He felt the scratch and tear of legs against his face; spindle-limbs which hooked the skin of lips and cheeks and fretted at the lids of his tightly closed eyes. The urgent thrust of abdomens bruised and coated with vented seed. It was impossible to breathe.

A dragging moment of nightmare in which he hung

helpless then, shifted by a vagrant gust of wind, the raft leveled, rising so as to support his weight.

"Earl!" The gust had cleared his ears. "Earl, help me!"

He heaved, dragging her body up and alongside his own, lifting her hand to the rail, releasing it when her fingers took hold. With his freed hand he swept the crawling bodies from his mouth and sucked air into his burning lungs. Only when he'd oxygenated his blood did he clear his eyes and look around.

Selina was beside him, eyes tightly closed beneath a scatter of ephemerae. They opened when he passed his hand over her face. The creatures had thinned now, the olive darkness replaced by a dull, emerald sheen which lightened even as he watched. The swarm, dissipating, riding the winds, expanding like smoke to streak the heavens with fading color.

Boyce had gone; thrown out when the raft had tilted and now lying dead and broken on the rocks below. Selina called out as Dumarest edged his way toward the vacant controls.

"Earl! Don't leave me!"

"Stay where you are and hang on tight."

Dumarest brushed ephemerae from his face. Beneath him the raft tilted again, veering, dropping to spin in a fluttering circle as if it had been a leaf blown from a tree. A descent which would smash both the craft and its occupants if unchecked. Dumarest increased his pace and reached the controls just as a fresh cloud of ephemerae closed about the machine.

A moment in which he was deafened, blinded, locked in a world of distorted movement. One which passed almost as quickly as it had come, leaving him fighting to maintain the stability of the raft, to set it down with a wrenching crash on jagged stones. A successful landing—he could walk away. But Selina was dying.

She lay two hundred yards from the wreck of the raft, a pale splotch against the ochre ground, her hair spread to form a curtain about her head. At first she seemed unharmed then Dumarest saw the unnatural angle of a leg, the rim of blood edging her lips, the dark mottling of ugly bruises on her side.

"Earl!" A hand lifted toward him as he headed to where she lay. "Earl, my darling—it hurts!"

The pain of torn muscle, wrenched sinews, broken bones and ruptured internal organs. Agony which would increase as the initial shock lessened. Gently he examined her, hearing the hiss of indrawn breath as he straightened the broken leg. The spleen, he guessed, certainly a kidney, and the back could be broken as was the collarbone. Injuries which could be cured given the right treatment but the raft was bereft of any emergency medical supplies and how to summon aid? And even if she could be moved to the house what then? Jarvis had no money and the surgery she needed would be expensive.

"Earl?" She looked at him as if guessing his thoughts. "Is it bad?"

"No."

"You're lying. I can't move my legs and my side is numb. It hurts when I breathe and I feel sick." She drew in her breath. "Damn!"

"There's nothing I can give you," he said. "The raft—"

"I know."

"If Boyce had done his job—"

"He's dead," she said. "And it wasn't really his fault. I should have hung on as you told me to but I freed a hand to wipe my face and the other slipped. It seemed a long way to fall."

A matter of a couple of hundred feet at the most, probably much less, but it had been enough. The rocks waiting to impact her body hadn't been gentle. Dumarest reached forward to wipe her face. She was sweating and blood seeped from between her lips. He could imagine her pain.

"Manna," she said. "Earl, get me some manna."

"What?"

"There." Her hand lifted, pointing. "Among the rocks. You'll see its shine. Hurry, Earl, please."

The sun was high and he turned her face before rising to search. The winds had dusted the ground and formed little dunes at the bases of jumbled rocks. Some of them shone with a crystal glitter and he knelt to gather the harvest; the empty bodies of male ephemerae, voided by their mating, dried by sun and wind, losing all color to gleam as if made of glass. They stirred as he blew away the dust, crumpled as he closed his fingers around them.

"Earl!" Selina was weakening, a victim of rising agony. "Hurry, Earl!"

His shadow fell over her face as he rejoined her, kneeling to put one hand beneath her head, lifting as he held the cupped palm of the other to her lips. Eagerly she tongued the small heap of substance into her mouth. A moment then, incredibly, she laughed.

"Wasn't it fun, Earl? I've never had a ride like it before. To go right into the color—fantastic!"

He said nothing, lifting the hair from her forehead, keeping the sun from her eyes.

"You look sad, my darling, but there's no need." Her hand moved to touch his own. "There's nothing to worry about. A few years—what am I losing? At least now I'll never grow old and ugly. In fact I'm looking forward to what is to come. Maybe we'll meet again, Earl. Go riding into more colors." She yawned. "God, I'm tired! I think I'll take a nap now. You'll stay with me, darling?"

"I'll stay."

A promise he kept until there was no further need.

Rising he looked down at the dead girl. Despite the blood her face was peaceful, the eyes closed, even the mouth seeming as if she smiled. Against the ochre sand her hair gleamed with the richness of oiled silk. Even as he watched an ephemera, a gravid female, scuttled from the loom of a rock to quest at its edge in search of a nesting site. It darted away from the moving shadow of his hand. Moved again as a second shadow came to rest beside his own.

"Earl!" Isobel Boulaye stood a few feet away, a half-loaded raft resting behind her. "I didn't know it was you. I saw your raft and came in search." Her eyes moved to the girl. "Dead?"

"Yes."

"Don't feel bad about it. There was nothing you could have done."

Nothing but to kill her with painless mercy, but the manna had taken care of that. Dumarest looked at the flecks clinging to his palm, remembering what Anna had given Estelle, the flitters he had drunk in wine. Lifting his hand he tongued the shining powder and tasted a familiar sweetness. Not a poison then, but what?

"A curse." The woman had been watching him. "The blight of this world, Earl. Most can't live without it, a few leave it alone, some are able to reject it. You could be one of them."

"And you?"

"I leave it alone. Did she?"

"No."

"A pity. She was so beautiful. Were you lovers?"

Dumarest looked at her knowing it was kinder to lie. "No."

"Earl—"

"We were friends," he said harshly. "We ran and swam and played games together. The last one killed her." He glanced to where her raft was standing. "If you have something to wrap around her and will give me transportation I'll take her back to her people." He frowned as she shook her head. "You refuse?"

"There are customs, Earl. On Elysius the dead lie where they fall and they do not lie for long. You understand?"

Predators, creatures which lurked beneath the sand, scavengers who lived on the dead—such were common on many worlds. Even the custom held merit—a return of sustenance to the land, but on this world it could hold a deeper significance. In the rising clouds of ephemerae she would live again. He wondered what color she would be.

Chapter NINE

———◆◉◆———

Anna was busy in the foyer when Dumarest entered the Argive House. "Earl! It's good to see you!" Her lips pursed as she studied his soiled clothing, bright metal gleaming through rips in the plastic. "Man, you look a mess! What did they do to you?" She shook her head when he'd told her. "That poor girl. What about you? From the look of it you need a hot bath and a massage."

Things offered by Isobel which he'd refused. "Where's Zalman?"

"Hans? He's out somewhere, but never mind about him. Get into the bath and leave your clothes outside." She turned, shouting, "Celia! Stoke up the boiler!" Then, to Dumarest. "Don't be a fool, Earl. Zalman can wait."

The water was steaming and Dumarest sank into it, conscious of aches and bruises from his legs, hips, and shoulder. The legs had taken the impact of the landing, transmitted shock jarring the tissues of the hips. He'd rolled when the raft had hit, slamming his shoulder hard against a rock, lucky not to have cracked his skull. The protective mesh buried in his garments had saved him from lacerations but the bone had been bruised.

He moved in the water, adding more hot to that inside the tub, leaning back and inhaling the moist vapor. Luck, again it had saved him, but for how much longer?

"Earl? Where are your clothes?"

He'd forgotten and watched as Celia came into the bathroom to collect them. She turned at the door, smiling, losing the smile as her mother yelled to her again. Alone Dumarest laved his body, washed off the suds, and refilled

93

the tub with fresh, near-boiling water. Heat which eased
the aches and would bring out the bruises. Anna was
waiting for him in the bedroom when he finally left the
tub.

"Sit." She gestured to his bed. "And you can get rid of
that towel. I've nursed enough men to know what they're
like."

He sat, retaining the towel, looking at the woman and
what she had brought with her. She had rolled her sleeves
to the elbows and had set a bottle of oil on the table
beside the bed. As he settled she handed him a goblet full
of steaming liquid.

"Tisane," she explained. "Herbs steeped in boiling
water and with a couple of extra ingredients to help. It'll
relax you and bring sleep." Then, as he hesitated, she
added, "There's no manna in it, that I swear. I don't use
the stuff. I saw what it did to the man who owned this
place, my parents, too many others. Drink up, Earl, and
let me work on those bruises."

He drank and stretched on the bed, feeling the towel
fall away as, palms filled with oil, the woman set about
massaging his body. She was skilled, strong fingers probing, following the line of muscle and sinew, easing, reliev-
ing tensions and dispersing nodes of discomfort. At her
command he turned and lay face down, one cheek against
the pillow, eyes closed, feeling himself drift as the tisane
took effect.

Reliving the events of the past few days, the laughing
pleasure he had known with Selina, the last ride, the fall.

Why had he been so careless?

The manna had been to blame; the saccharin sweetness
culled from the dead ephemerae robbing him of all sense
of urgency. It had turned the days into a succession of
pleasant interludes in which time had no meaning. He saw
Selina's face again, heard her laughter, her utter indiffer-
ence to death. An armor won after he had fed her the
crystal glitters.

A curse, Isobel had called it. The blight of this world,
but it could not always have been that. The houses had
been built to last, the town, the settlement as a whole.

One more fortunate than most for the manna would have provided a food rich in protein, easily gathered and easily stored. A guarantee of personal freedom for every man, woman, and child. Together with the mild climate it would have been enough to have eliminated the more savage aspects of survival. There would have been time for pursuing the arts, personal relationships, the enjoyment of pleasure. Then the world would have been blessed with happiness.

But something had happened. When?

Dumarest turned, easing his bruises. Anna had said she'd arrived on Elysius when young—forty years ago at the most. The delapidation of the houses could have taken that long. The erosion of morale would have been faster but say forty years. It would have started slowly, insidiously; a subtle mutation of the ephemerae which changed the manna from a harmless, slightly invigorating food into something far more complex. Something which quelled natural caution, gave a lasting euphoria, changed the perspective and altered the appreciation of time. A window needs to be repaired? I'll do it tomorrow. A door to be put back on its hinges—tomorrow. An electronic circuit to be fixed—tomorrow. Tomorrow, always tomorrow, a tomorrow which never came.

He turned again and saw Selina smiling at him, the blood on her mouth the ruby of crushed roses, the mane of her hair the limitless ocean of space, the glitter of dead bodies, the stars which shone like lanterns in the empty dark.

Stars which were suns accompanied by worlds of endless variety.

Which of them all was the one he sought?

A lonely world far out to the rim, one circled by a great silver moon, a planet scarred and torn by ancient cataclysms. The planet of his birth and the only home he could ever know. Finding it was the reason for his existence.

In sleep he was there again, small, cold, huddled against a rock, watching the ship which had landed, its strange markings bright in the wash of moonlight. An open hatch and the desperation which drove him toward it. Darkness and a place in which he had hid. The hum and sense of movement and, after a long while, the discovery when he had ventured out to search for food.

Like water shivered in a pool, images passed before him; the captain's face, the ship, the fear, the sick knowledge of what could happen, the stars which shone hungrily waiting for him to be evicted. And then other worlds, long journeys leading always toward the heart of the galaxy. New captains, new ships, fresh worlds as he grew and became a man. A lifetime compressed into whirling depictions but, always, remained his need to find Earth.

Tomorrow—he would find it tomorrow.

It was dusk when he woke and he lay like an animal, conscious that he was not alone. Zalman stood beside the bed, stooped over the cleaned and refurbished clothing heaped on a chair. He straightened as Dumarest watched to look through the window. The light made him look old and tense; a man unsure of himself, one afraid.

"Hans?"

"You're awake!" He spun, smiling. "I'm glad you're back, Earl. Anna told me what happened. I brought up your clothes." He gestured toward them. "She did a good job. God, man, you could have been killed!"

"Why didn't you warn me?"

"About the manna?" Zalman made no effort to pretend he didn't understand. "I didn't know, Earl. I just didn't know."

The stuff had rotted the world for decades—how could he have been ignorant?

"Please!" Zalman had read Dumarest's anger, his disbelief. "I've never been here before, Earl. Don't you understand? I'm as much a stranger as you are. No!" He backed, one hand lifting as Dumarest rose from the bed. "I'm not lying, Earl."

"You told me you knew someone. A man here on Elysius!"

"That's true but, Earl, never did I tell you I'd ever been here."

"You told Julie she would be wasting her time opening a house."

"That was also true—but I was working on information I'd gathered. The gambler knew her intentions and thought her a fool. The steward—it was like reading a warning notice."

"The manna?"

"Nothing, Earl, I swear it. By the time I'd learned of the danger you'd left with Estelle. I tried to contact you but no one at the house bothered to answer."

A possibility—the Hausi could have a special method of gaining attention, and now the matter was of no importance. But the reason he had come to Elysius still remained.

Dumarest said, "The man you swore knew of Earth. Where is he?"

"Earl, I didn't lie. I met him before he came here and he had the answer. It meant nothing to me then, just an odd item of information, but he had it, of that I'm certain." He added, "It was on Ascelius when—"

"Ascelius! His name?"

He knew it before Zalman told him and felt again the old, familiar pain. Too late—must he always be too late? Rudi Boulaye was dead, buried in the hills—had his secret died with him?

Isobel Boulaye said, "Earl, I'm so very glad you called. Your friend, too." Her eyes moved to where Zalman stood beside the raft now grounded on the roof. "As I told you I am never visited."

"Since Rudi died?"

"Even before. There is a lack of social life on this world as you must have learned by now. It didn't bother us—our own company was enough."

"If we are inconveniencing you please say so." An empty courtesy, if she had knowledge he would gain it, but there was no need to be either brusque or impolite. "But I do need to talk to you."

A need, she hoped, equal to her own. The day had been a torment with his presence constantly with her—his

arrival a totally unexpected delight. From where he sat at
the controls of the raft Mtouba said, "Well, if they can
stay I'll be off. My regards, Madam Boulaye. Good luck,
Earl."

As the vehicle lifted she said, "What did he mean?"

Dumarest smiled at her expression. "I may have given
him a false impression in order to win his help in getting
out here. I mentioned your mine and that I've worked as
a miner. As an agent he is anxious to see your shipments
increased."

"For the sake of his commission." She nodded, knowing it was more than that. "Are you?"

"A miner?"

"Yes. Have you worked in mines? Do you know about
them? If so would you—" She broke off, conscious of
being carried away. Slowly, it was best to move slowly—
how often had Rudi advised that? "Let's go down into the
house."

The night was thickening, stars blossoming over the
hills, and she shivered as she headed toward the stairs. A
shiver born more of emotion than climate and she fought
to maintain her self-control. She was a grown woman, not
an impressionable adolescent, and surely she could entertain two guests to dinner without making a fool of herself?

"You've caught me unawares," she said as she guided
them into the lounge. "There's food, naturally, but my
cook is somewhat erratic. If you'll be patient I'll prepare
something myself. While I'm doing it help yourself to
wine. That machine produces music, that some pleasing
colors or—" She hesitated then decided against showing
them Rudi's drawings. Not yet. Not ever unless he
showed interest. "Just make yourself at home."

After she'd left Zalman said, "She's tense, Earl. Anxious."

"Afraid?"

"No. She wants you to do something. It could be to
take her husband's place." He added, casually, "You realize she is in love with you?"

Love or desire? Had Selina loved him or had it been a
game? Words used to enhance emotion and to stimulate

desire yet those same words, used between others under the same circumstances, could hold such a greater depth of meaning.

Dumarest said, "Anything else?"

"Nothing sharp or clear as yet. That is to be expected, she is disturbed, flustered. She wanted to show you something then decided against it. She was on the verge of asking you something then decided to wait. Give it time, Earl, let her settle."

Have patience—wait! Advice he found hard to follow. One question could resolve his doubts yet the timing of that question was all-important. Had the man confided in his wife? Did she share the secret? Would she divulge it? And, if guessing its value, would she ask a price he couldn't pay?

Dumarest rose, like the woman he needed something to occupy his attention. She was busy in the kitchen and he moved toward the devices she had mentioned, activating one, listening to a succession of tonal chords which irritated rather than pleased. Rudi's choice? The color organ was little better and he turned from it after juggling with the controls. Appreciation of the glowing hues depended on mood and his was far from appropriate.

"Here!" Zalman had occupied himself with the profered refreshment. "Have some wine."

Dumarest took it, studying the lambent violet, finding it free of betraying glitters. The taste was of lemon and thyme. Lowering the glass he looked at the chamber.

"Neglected," said Zalman, reading him. "Like everything else in the house, I guess, but what can you expect? A lone woman trying to do it all. God knows why she doesn't sell up and get out."

"Because I can't." She had joined them as he spoke. "Because no one wants to buy. How can you work a mine without labor and who wants to dig when a handful of manna provides everything you need? I've servants only because they're too damned lazy to fend for themselves. Workers only because they've run out of manna and are willing to eat my food and scratch at the dirt until the devils dance again and when they do they forget why they are where they are. A curse, Earl, as I told you. This used to be a thriving, commercial world at one time. Then, with no exports, the ships stopped coming. Soon there won't even be a Hausi resident here and, when he goes, that'll be the end. Those who are left will sit and grin and play and pass the hours like happy children. Like idiots!"

"No!" Zalman was sharp. "You had it right the first time. Why does a man work? To feed himself and his family and what else? To obtain those things he is told are necessary to his status and comfort: a house, a means of transportation, clothing, toys, special foods—the list is as long as commercial interests can make it. And those who rule him always have a hand extended for taxes. Here there is none of that. A man eats the manna and he is happy. Can Heaven offer more?"

She said, "Earl—is that how you think?"

"Hans asked a question. Can you answer it?" Then, as she remained silent, Dumarest added, "Each to his own, Isobel. To you these people are idiots, to others they have all anyone could want. It all depends on your point of view."

"And yours?"

"Mine is simple—live and let live." He finished his wine. "Dare I ask if the food is ready?"

The meal was plain; dehydrated foods mixed, blended, cooked in the microwave oven and garnished with hastily prepared sauces. A meal Rudi would have disdained but which her guests ate with relish. Toying with her own she thought about what Dumarest had said.

To live and let live.

A simple philosophy but great truths were always simple. She remembered the discussions she'd had with Rudi in the past when the full impact of the mistake he'd made had registered. How he had wanted to alter the ecology of this world with men and machines hired to destroy the ephemerae with radioactive dusts, flame, and poisons. To rob the population of their manna so as to force them to work—to dig in the mine, to provide the wealth he lacked. Riches he professed to despise yet for which he inwardly yearned. Why else did he delve for precious metal? Why else expound his dream?

She had agreed with him then—did she agree with him now? The girl who had died had probably known more pure enjoyment in her few short years than both she and Rudi in their combined lifetimes. And, if life had any purpose at all, wasn't it to be enjoyed?

"Madam?" Zalman, watching, leaned forward to replenish her glass. "You were introspective," he said. "Thoughtful. Recalling an incident in the past, maybe?"

"My husband." She pushed aside her plate. "He loved good food, wine, conversation. I am not doing his memory credit."

"Because of the meal?" He shook his head, smiling. "Simple food nicely served, what could be better? You agree, Earl?"

"The meal was excellent," said Dumarest. "As you're thinking of your late husband let's talk about him. That is, if it will cause you no pain. No? Then where did you meet? On Ascelius?"

"Yes. He taught at the university. I was a student. I'd known him for years but we didn't get close until I returned for a post-graduate degree in geology. I was the oldest in the class and that was enough to bring me to his attention. We shared a few meals and saw a few plays and then, well, it just happened."

"You married?"

"Yes." She paused, remembering, a little surprised at the lack of pain. "Then, well, Rudi was always a dreamer and he'd heard about Elysius. The wealth which was just waiting to be won. It's true, too, there is wealth here; the Fulden Hills are loaded with jascar." She ended, bitterly, "Getting it is something else."

Zalman poured more wine. He said, "I met your husband. It must have been about the time you were going together. There was a celebration—the Lupinia?"

"The Ludernia. Yes, we'd just started going out together then." Seven years ago—was it so long? "We married that same year and came to Elysius the year after."

"So I heard. Did he ever mention me?" Zalman

shrugged as she shook her head. "It doesn't matter. It's just that we shared a love of old things; stories, legends, things like that. He told me he had evidence of the actual existence of a mythical planet. Did he ever mention it? The planet Earth?"

A casual question placed by a master and Dumarest fought the instinctive clenching of his hand as he waited for the reply.

"Earth?" Isobel frowned. "No, I don't think so. A planet, you say? What an odd name."

"It has another," said Dumarest. "Terra. Did he ever mention a world named that?"

"No. No, I don't think so." She rose, bustling to clear away the dishes. "If you'd care to return to the lounge I'll bring in the tisane. Or would you prefer coffee? I think there's some around if the cook hasn't used it all. Or there could be something else."

"Tisane will do," said Zalman quickly. "The one Rudi liked—you don't mind me calling him by name? In a sense I've known him as long as yourself."

"No, Hans, I don't mind." How good it was to be on friendly terms again with mutual friends. "He liked it spiced and hotly pungent. Earl?"

"The same, please, Isobel."

In the lounge Zalman said, quietly, "Keep her mind on her husband. I caught something, a hint, my guess is she knows but is not wholly aware of what she knows. The man must have talked and told her what he suspected or had discovered. It may not have registered—a new bride would have other things on her mind than legendary worlds. Just be patient."

A game in which he held all the cards; knowing if and when she lied, told the truth or what she thought was the truth, held back, hesitated, stilled unspoken questions. Dumarest watched as the man went to meet Isobel when she entered the room, the way he relieved her of her burden, poured the steaming tisane, sipped, nodded with false appreciation.

"Just as I remembered. Rudi liked strong flavors. Why did he yield his position at the university?"

"For me." She shrugged at his expression. "I was twenty years his junior and he was conscious of the disparity. A little guilty, I think, though he had no reason. He wanted to give me the universe as a reward for having been so kind as to become his wife. Stupid, of course, but it pleased him so I didn't argue. Then, one day, he told me we were coming here. He was like a boy and full of grandiose ideas. We would gather wealth and use it to go to a place where we would find riches beyond all imagining. It was all nonsense. Just foolish talk."

"No," said Dumarest. "He could—" He fell silent as Zalman lifted a warning hand.

"Talk," he murmured. "And maybe foolish, but not wholly so. After all he did yield his position and come to Elysius. That couldn't have been cheap."

"It took all we had," she admitted.

"And yet, loving you as he did, still he came."

"To die. To be buried."

"But he left something behind? A chest, some papers, a journal?" Zalman's eyes were shrewd as he read her answer. "He did?"

"There are some drawings. He made them when making a survey of the hills."

"But there's more," urged Zalman. "Things he brought with him from Ascelius. Books? Graphs? Condensed computer readouts? A file?" He nodded as if she had spoken. "It could hold the answer to your problem, my dear. Rudi was not a fool and I am certain he would never have risked your future security without excellent reason. If we could see that file?"

He relaxed as she left the room. "Earl, my friend, I think we have it."

Dumarest looked at his cup of tisane. The surface of the untouched liquid was quivering, alive with dancing coruscations of reflected light, the cup and fluid acting as an amplifier to magnify the trembling of his hand. He set it down and the surface stilled and grew calm. An example he found impossible to follow.

The secret at last?

Was the woman, even now, fetching him the information he had searched for so long? The coordinates which would signal the place in the galaxy where Earth was to be found? The figures which were carried in no almanac, no navigation table no matter how old. Figures which had to exist and yet were absent.

"Here!" Isobel was back, a thick folder in her hands, one stamped with the seal of the university on Ascelius. "He called this his treasure chest—I've no idea why and when I asked him to explain it to me once he grew annoyed. It wasn't worth pursuing the matter. If Rudi wanted to keep a secret I saw no harm in it and we all need some privacy. I've never even opened it."

"Not even after he'd died?"

"No, Earl." She met his eyes. "He could have had things in there from his past. Details I wouldn't have wanted to know about."

The photographs of previous loves, evidence of a side of his nature never revealed, data of weaknesses she hadn't wanted to expose. Dumarest wondered at her sensitivity then remembered how late she had married and to whom. Had Rudi been a father image and had she wanted to remain deliberately blind to any faults? Or had the rejection of the file been a part of her closing her mind against the agonies of the past? The dead were dead—let the dead rest in peace. The man, the love, the memories, the hopes—lock them all behind a closed door.

He looked at the folder she'd placed in his hands. It was fastened by a clasp of cheap gilded metal and he thumbed it open. It was fashioned after a box; loose leaves placed within, a spring to hold them firm. A scent of dust rose when he opened it, a musty odor containing the hint of decay.

"Earl?"

Dumarest ignored the other man. The topmost paper was covered with a mass of neat handwriting and he read it, words and phrases seeming to spring from the sheet, to glow as if illuminated . . . Earth . . . Terra . . . The Original People.

He read on:

The Original People are a minor sect of religious fanatics to be found on various backward planets scattered throughout the galaxy. The sect is a secret one and does not seek nor welcomes converts; fresh followers being obtained from the natural increase of existing worshippers. The main tenet of their belief is that Mankind originated on a single world, the mythical planet Earth, and that, after cleansing by trial and tribulation, Mankind will return to this supposed world of origin at which time the universe will cease to exist and the cleansed race be transformed into a higher form of life. This belief, founded on an obvious fallacy, is surrounded by esoteric ritual and elaborate ceremonies based on a primitive cult of fertility. There are no grounds for supporting the truth of their contention which must remain as one of the more illogical creeds.

(Extract from "Rites and Rituals of the Romantic." Vol. 3 University Library Ascelius)

Note 12: The assumption that the mythical planet cannot exist because the beliefs surrounding it are patently absurd is a clear example of irrational thinking and demonstrably untrue. See TERRA, *note 28.*

Dumarest rippled papers, oblivious to the others.

Terra is an alternate name for Earth and could have an association with the creed of the Original People which states—From terror they fled to find new places on which to expiate their sins. Only when cleansed will the race of Man be again united.

Note 28: The name tends to bolster the belief of the creed but could be a natural distortion. It does, however, lend weight to the possibility of an actual planet existing and which has, somehow, become forgotten. Discounting the obvious fallacies of the

*belief expressed by the religious sect the similarity of
name remains together with the undeniable association of a place left and waiting to be discovered. If
we accept that legends are messages forwarded from
one generation to another, said messages becoming
distorted with the passage of time and repetition, together with the necessity of making such messages
simple to begin with, we see the possibility that the
creed does hold, in its heart, the knowledge of a
world known as Earth.*

There was more, much more, and Dumarest read it all.
The hints that Earth was a repository of vast wealth. That
it was made of solid metal all precious. That it was an artificial construction housing technological knowledge of
unbelievable magnitude—all snares which had trapped
Rudi Boulaye and had cost him his life.

Yet the man had believed.

And the man had known.

He had *known!*

"Earl!" This time Zalman wasn't to be denied. "It's
there, isn't it? The answer. I've kept my promise. More
than kept it. Not the man, true, but what he'd learned.
My share of our partnership."

Isobel said, "Is that what you wanted, Earl? The coordinates of a world?"

"Yes."

"And do you have it?"

"No."

Zalman reared to his feet. "Earl, you—" He broke off,
reading the truth. "No," he said, dully. "It can't be. Look
again, man, look again."

There was no need and Zalman's despair was nothing
against his own disappointment. Dumarest leaned back,
seeing again the papers he had read, the dry expositions
couched in precise words and bearing the stamp of the
man of letters. A lecturer who had put down his thoughts,
the steps which had led to his final discovery—and yet he
had not written down the essential data.

Why not?

And why should the file contain a receipt from a jeweler?

Dumarest looked at it. "Isobel, did Rudi wear a ring?"

"No."

"No other jewelry? Did he give you a piece." He handed her the receipt. "A ring or necklace, perhaps?"

"No." She studied the paper. "This must be for the chain and medallion he wore around his neck. I remember now. I wondered why he had bought it. He'd never worn anything like it before. When I asked him about it he laughed and said he wore our future around his neck. I thought he was joking—Earl! Your face—is something wrong?"

A man playing games, hugging to himself the secret he had won, the discovery he had made. A man given to flights of imagination who'd given free rein to his fantasy. Dumarest could almost see him buying the medallion, stamping it with the precious coordinates, wearing it around his neck. A secret safe from prying eyes—one now buried with him far below the Fulden Hills.

Chapter TEN

———•◉•———

Axilia was cleaning gutters when Dumarest arrived back at the tavern. He'd begun work early; the day was barely bright with dawn, gold and orange tinging the azure, reflecting from the fluffy clouds which had gathered far out over the sea. Later, perhaps, the air would tinge with color but now it was clear.

"Sven!"

The miner looked down at the call. He stood high on a ladder, a bucket hooked to the rungs, a trowel in one hand. He was stripped to the waist and was smeared with a thick, black mud.

"Sven, can we talk?"

"Just a minute."

Axilia returned to his task, scooping sediment from the gutter and dropping it into the bucket. A pile of the rich dirt standing to one side told of his labors. Only when the container was filled did he descend, holding it in one hand. Silently he emptied it, adding to the existing pile, then, as if steeling himself, he looked at Dumarest.

"Well?"

"How's the nose?"

It was swollen, a little red but otherwise normal. A few more days and it would be wholly healed. The bruise on the temple had also faded.

Axilia said, "Is that what you've come to talk about?"

"Our fight? No. I just want to know if you figure it ended. Is it?"

"The damned thing was a mistake, Earl. I was drunk, crazed I guess, you know how it can be. That woman—I

108

was wrong." He sounded as if pleased to make the admission. "Anna told me what happened—she figures you could have killed me."

"How are you getting on with her?"

"Anna? I'm in her debt and am working to clear it. The gutters, the roof, some internal stuff. She offered me a deal. I guess she offered you the same one."

"She did. Did you take it?"

"No. I want to look around first. From what I can make out there's work for a willing man. Maybe I can find it at some of the big estates." He looked past Dumarest at the raft he'd arrived in. "I see you've managed to get fixed up."

"In a way. Are you still interested in mining?" Dumarest read the answer. "Good. Any objection to working for a woman? The one you tried to kill?" Then, as the man hesitated, he added, "She bears no grudge, Sven, but I guess you owe it to her. Right?"

The miner nodded. "What's the proposition?"

Dumarest explained after the man had cleaned up and they sat with steaming mugs of tisane. Anna, if she guessed he was stealing her labor, had made no comment but, noticing how the man's eyes followed her, Dumarest guessed the reason for her apparent unconcern. There were more ways to hold a man than with food and wine. Often the promise of something more intimate was enough, a hint of future union and Sven, despite his face, was a well-built man.

Now he frowned at the drawings Dumarest had spread on the table before them.

"This the layout?" He scowled as Dumarest nodded. "Amateur work—it's got the brand. These damned fools think all you need to do to mine is dig a few holes in the ground. What's the substrata? Limestone? Sandstone? Shale? If it's real hard rock you'll be in trouble unless you've the equipment and men." He studied the maps again. "Jascar, you say?"

"Yes." Dumarest held out his hand. "Here."

It was the scrap Rudi had held when he'd died and Axilia examined it, digging at it with a blunt thumbnail. The metal was blue, soft, malleable the mark made by his nail clearly visible. He hefted it, judging its weight, pursing his lips as he set it down.

"Has much been taken out as yet?"

"No."

"Good." Axilia poked at the small nugget. "This could have come from the main deposit. You ever mined this stuff? It rests in nodes in strata where the conditions were right for its formation. Don't ask me how it's made, I don't know and I don't think anyone does. I heard a man say once that it could be the result of some local but intensive force such as a field-drive applied from a ship landing or leaving—high pressure coupled with electronic intensity—but that's just speculation. The thing is it forms a central cluster with particles widely scattered around it. If you hit the external particles you have to delve beyond them to the main deposit. If they haven't taken much from the mine it could still be there."

"Waiting to be collected?"

"Maybe." Axilia was grim. "But getting it won't be easy. The strata is usually unstable and the biggest danger is from shifting stresses causing falls and cave-ins. I know of three juscar mines where the stuff is still there just waiting to be collected but no one can get to it without paying more than it's worth. Labor," he explained. "Equipment. Tools and time. Some sharp operators sell claims to suckers—they're genuine enough but worthless if you know what it's all about."

And Rudi hadn't. A man blinded by a dream and killed by his own ignorance.

Dumarest said, "What's your answer, Sven?"

Axilia hesitated, looking again at the plans, frowning as he assessed the possibilities. "A share if I get out the juscar, right?"

"Right."

"And a free hand? I don't want any woman telling me how to handle my job. Sorry, Earl, I know I owe her, but that's how it is. The shafts go where I direct and are built as I say." He added, "But who do we have to build them?"

"You, me, Zalman. How about the others? Ochen? Quail? Tocsaw? Think they'll be interested?"

"In shares? Maybe. Anyone else?"

"The woman has men who sometimes work but they're unreliable. It's possible there could be others in town who could use some real money." Details which rested on the miner's acceptance of the proposition; without his skill and experience the project was hopeless. Dumarest said, casually, "Of course, if the work seems too much, you can always hit the manna."

"Not me!"

"Why not? No worries if you do. Just eat some of the stuff and every day's a holiday. You won't care about a thing; your face, the way you dress, the way you live. And it's free. Just go out and pick it up by the handful. It's easy."

Axilia said, "Quit needling me, Earl. You mentioned my face but you don't know how I got it. A woman, yes, and acid, but I was doped at the time, riding high. A damned fool, but I learned. Being a zombie is no way to live. Anna—" He broke off then said, quietly, "She's a good woman, Earl, and a man could do worse than stay with her. With money I could get my face fixed and maybe—well, it's worth the chance."

Dumarest made no comment, watching as again the man studied the drawings, this time with a different attitude. The criticism was there still but now there was something more; a judgment, an assessment, a tenuous program of progress to be instigated. A blunt finger traced a detail.

"This must have been the original shaft, right?"

"So Isobel told me. It was there when they came."

"An old working, tried and abandoned." The finger moved on. "This the second? I guessed so. Another failure; the angle and direction are all to hell. This produced metal, right?"

"Some."

"But not much. They were working through the periphery." Again the finger moved to another section. "Here?"

"A blocked tunnel." The one where Rudi was buried and Dumarest's main target. "It could lead to the nexus."

"What makes you say that?" Axilia pursed his lips as he listened. "He came out with this in his hand?" He touched the nugget and again examined it. "You could be right. What do you suggest?"

To clear the tunnel, find the body, get what hung around its neck and then win what could be found. The only way to recover the secret Rudi Boulaye had discovered.

Dumarest said, "Maybe we could open it—the woman would like to bury her husband's body back on his home world."

"That needn't be easy," said Axilia. "It could even be impossible; if the strata is slipping the shaft will fill as fast as it's cleared. Maybe we could drive in at an angle just beyond and work back to find the line. I'll have to study the terrain." He stared at Dumarest. "Well? When do we start?"

On Liment a cyber had died; burned in a palace fired by a rioting mob. A loss but one the man himself should have been able to avoid and his failure to predict the uprising had held its own punishment. The incident on Chierene was different; there a young and spoiled daughter of a tycoon had slashed a servant of the Cyclan across the face with her whip.

Elge studied the report and decided on what action was necessary. The services of the Cyclan to be withdrawn immediately with no compensatory return of fees. The cyber in question to be reassigned. Instructions given to weigh the balance in favor of the tycoon's rivals. The man would be ruined and he would know who was to blame. His anger against the girl would be far more telling than any other form of punishment.

And the news would spread.

Alone that would help to strengthen the respect in which cybers were held and increase the deference shown them by rulers and commoners alike. An armor, invisible but real, a defense against anger and pride and a guarantee of the immunity which was the basis of real power. To strike at a cyber was to strike at the Cyclan itself. To demean the part was to demean the whole. A lesson which must be taught whenever necessary, not as a matter of revenge but of expediency.

Elge glanced at the next report; a matter of general guidance as to the progress of expansion in a remote part of the galaxy. It could continue as at present; to advance expansion too fast on too many fronts would be to risk a lessening of efficiency. Other matters followed; decisions to be made which he settled with smooth ability. Promotions to be ratified, new clients to be approved.

Data which he received as a matter of finalization but which to ignore was to invite a gradual erosion of power and the possibility of accumulated error. A decision made by a cyber could be valid in the light of his limited knowledge, wrong in the overall scheme of things. The organization, like a machine, needed its governors and safety devices, its checks and counterchecks.

"Master?" The communicator hummed with the smooth monotone. "Councillor Boule as expected."

"Show him in."

A distraction but one to be borne. Cyber Boule was more fanatical than most in his determination to stamp out any trace of inefficiency, and to ignore him was to be more than inefficient. It was as important to maintain harmony with the Council as to direct the workings of the great plan.

"Councillor." Elge rose to greet him. "You are welcome. The matter of Elysius, of course."

Boule was direct. "Time and effort has been expended in a pursuit which is patently illogical. Neither of the two affected units has had any connection with anything named Elysius yet you ordered the technicians to investigate worlds of that and similar names."

"That is so."

"The reason escapes me."

Elge said, "I am covering every possibility no matter how apparently remote. The word is the only clue we have as to what could have affected the catatonic unit.

Nequal's sacrifice must not be wasted. That is why I have ordered cybers together with acolytes to travel to, and report on, each of those worlds."

"Twelve of them."

"Each bearing a name which could be a derivation of the clue word: Lysius, Eylsius, Silysus—you must have the complete list." He added, "The total was arrived at only after the most thorough elimination."

"And your prediction as to the probability of success?"

"Low," admitted Elge. "But even if the probability were no higher than one tenth of one per cent I would regard the effort justified."

"Perhaps, but I doubt if the Council will agree. Waste must not be tolerated. Your method of operation is too similar to blasting an area with missiles rather than using one, carefully aimed, to hit the target. If there was one single factor associating either of the affected units to any of the worlds in question your action would be acceptable. As it is, there is the question of motive to be considered. I must warn you that the Council may ask you to justify your conduct."

An official notice of impending condemnation. As Cyber Prime he could ignore it if he wished but, if he should display such arrogance, he would prove that he was not fitted for the position he held. If nothing the Cyclan was a gestalt: the individual counted for little against the whole. Personal love of power, ambition, aggrandizement—all were concepts alien to any cyber. They worked and existed for the benefit of the whole.

Alone Elge activated the depicted galaxy and looked at the blaze of glowing motes. Nequal's toy and he could understand the fascination it had held for the man. There was a soothing quality about it, a hypnotic attraction so that, as he stood watching, it seemed that he encompassed the entire universe and that all the suns and worlds of creation were but cells of his corporal being.

An illusion, gone in a moment, but some of the heady intoxication remained. The sheer mental euphoria of grandiose design and one which held an insidious danger. Elge recognized it and, by the mere fact of recognition, negated it. He was not a god. He was not greater than the whole. He was no more than a cog in the complex machine of the Cyclan and, already, he had been warned he could be at fault.

Why had he ordered the investigation of those worlds?

Boule had been correct; there was no logical reason for the expenditure of such effort and, watching the model of the galaxy, he evaluated the steps which had led to his decision. He had been tired and the toxins accumulated by fatigue had affected the efficiency of his metabolism. That he had not postponed making the decision was a proof of his failure to acknowledge the circumstance and one which would tell against him if the Council chose to question his ability. And yet, with all the facts before him, he had still gone against the dictates of logic.

A higher order of mental association?

It was possible and tempting as an answer. Facts could be barriers as well as guide if those facts were based on restricted knowledge. It was a "fact" that men couldn't fly—yet with the aid of machines they could move from world to world. Other examples were legion but one was enough to illustrate the point. Had his mind, fogged with weariness, made an intuitive connection which now defied analysis?

Elysius—why Elysius?

It glowed before him, enhanced by electronic magic, a mote set against the fleck of its sun. Even at full enlargement it would gain no further detail; the scale was far too small for that. Only the position could be determined and Elge studied it together with the suns close by. Near to them loomed the dark mass of the Rift which had initiated Nequal's downfall.

Dumarest had been located there and should have been trapped. Instead he had moved on to land finally on Harge. The world on which he had died when trapped in a web of sand. Died—the prediction had been as close to certainty as any cyber dared to make. And his death had sealed Nequal's fate.

As his own fate would be sealed if his belief that the world of Elysius held the answer to the crying brain was wrong. But, unlike his predecessor, Elge knew he would be given no second chance.

Mtouba said, patiently, "You can't have the bracelet, my dear. You know that."

"Why not?" The woman was young and had the guileless eyes of a child. "It's pretty."

"Very pretty, but you have no credit."

"You can trust me."

"Of course, and I do, as I hope you trust me to hold the bracelet until you bring me something of value." He ushered the girl from his premises then turned to smile at Dumarest. "They're like children, Earl. They see something which shines and they want it." His eyes moved to the raft lying outside: Isobel's vehicle. "I see you came to an arrangement with Madam Boulaye."

"Yes."

"I'm glad for her. That woman has worked hard and gained little return. Some refreshment? Tisane? A liqueur? Or would you prefer this?"

Dumarest looked at the box the Hausi extended, the glitters it held. "No."

"Good. I'd wondered." The agent closed the box with a snap and threw it to lie with other items on his desk. The gloom thickened as he closed the door, brightened as he switched on a light. "A bad thing about Selina."

"How did Jarvis take it?"

"With dignity and with pain but he is old and knows that all things are transitory. I said that she and Boyce died instantly. It would be a kindness to let him continue to believe that."

"I doubt if I'll see him again."

"No, it is unlikely." Mtouba stood, waiting, "Is that what you came to ask?"

"I'm curious about the ships which call here. Traffic, I assume, isn't heavy."

"An obvious conclusion. The *Phril* has a sister ship, the *Mercador* and they operate in opposed directions. Mtouba moved his finger in a rough circle over his desk, the tip touching a succession of objects. "Think of these things as worlds. Both ships serve them at more or less regular intervals. Others could be traveling across." His hand swept over the circle. "Sometimes they will call if carrying passengers or a delivery. I usually get some notice—about a day."

A Hausi could be trusted and they never lied which was not to say they always told the complete and literal truth. The inference was that the machine he'd gestured to was a short-range affair but the supra hi-beam radio could have reached the far end of the galaxy.

Dumarest said, "Why do they call at all? What has Elysius to offer?" He followed Mtouba's eyes as they shifted to the box. "Manna?"

"Terminal institutions on local worlds have a use for it. It's cheap, effective and enables the hopelessly sick and aged to die without care—people like the woman you saw harvest it for me. The profits are small but the trade is regular."

Dumarest said, "You have your regular suppliers?"

"Of course, but—"

"Old residents, naturally. They deserve preference." He drew a list of names from a pocket and handed it to the agent. "These people might try to earn money that way. I'd appreciate it if you'd refuse to accommodate them."

Mtouba frowned at the list. "You've put down the men you arrived with and others who recently landed."

"Anna gave me their names. She's cooperating by refusing all credit. Ochen, for example, he's been living it up at the Argive House. Now he's found himself a woman, a young girl, and she'll want new clothes and trinkets. He might think to pay for them with manna."

"And Quail?" Mtouba nodded, understanding. "You hope to squeeze them, force them to work for you at the mine. But what of my profit? New arrivals bring in the biggest loads. Am I to tell them that I don't want the manna? To reduce my shipments? Where's the gain in that?"

"The gain will be in the juscar they collect," said Dumarest. "Your commission on that will more than cover any lost profits on the manna." He added, casually, "There will, of course, be a bonus."

"Of course—and if no Juscar is found?" Mtouba shrugged without waiting for an answer. "A gamble but one which appeals to me. The loss of a small but certain profit against a potentially large commission. My friend, you are subtle. At no cost to yourself you have done your best to ensure a supply of labor. I salute you."

Dumarest matched his smile, accepting the flattery and knowing just what it was worth. The agent would lose nothing—others could harvest the manna—but he stood to gain from any juscar which might be found. A bribe to tempt his further cooperation.

As the man poured wine he said, "On checking the workings I find there is an old tunnel. It was cut with a machine. Do you know what happened to it?"

"No." The agent handed Dumarest the small glass and lifted his own. "To a happy association!"

"To mutual profit!"

They drank and set down the glasses; a ceremony which Dumarest had experienced before and which Mtouba, on this backward world, had been eager to conduct. A salute to each other's commercial prowess and a bargain sealed. But Dumarest wasn't yet finished.

"The tunnel," he said. "According to Isobel you've supplied hand tools and some explosives together with drilling modules and various other items such as lamps, testers, sonic probes—there's no need to go through the list. But no heavy mining machinery."

"That is correct." Mtouba answered the unspoken question. "They couldn't pay for it. I tried to warn them of the local difficulties but, at first, the man wouldn't listen. Even so I managed to restrain his expenditure a little by working on the principle that more supplies should be paid for out of profits. A waste of time. As I had to remind Madam Boulaye the last load of supplies were all she could expect until her credit was replenished."

"If she should choose to sell?"

"Who would buy? The deed to the mine is worthless. Her house has some value, true, and I may be able to raise a little on the raft and other portable goods, but the total value will be small. On Elysius there are more houses than people—you have examined the town. Her only real chance is to find a buyer with no conception of local conditions."

An optimistic fool as Rudi had been. One whom she would be willing to rob. Dumarest looked through the window toward the town, a dying place as the agent had said; the manna must contain a sterilizing agent. But they had wandered far enough from the point.

He said, "Were you here when the mine was first opened?"

"No, that was before my time."

"So you've no idea what happened to the machinery." Dumarest looked thoughtful. "It's possible it could still be here. Tucked away in one of the warehouses, perhaps. Shall we take a look?"

They found it beneath a bundle of scented reeds; stalks dried to a brittle fragility, crumbling to powder as Dumarest threw them to one side. Mtouba sneezed, the lamp he held throwing a dancing beam over the walls and interior struts of the warehouse. It settled on the shape Dumarest had revealed.

It was dusty, neglected, metal dull where it should have been bright, edges blunt where they should have been sharp. Jagged metal showed broken components and protective paint had scabbed and peeled from joints and linkages.

"I should employ you, Earl. It will be in the books, of course, but who would think to look?" The circle of brilliance moved as Mtouba shone his light on one point after another. "The original owners must have lost heart or run out of capital. This machine could have been held against outstanding debt. Maybe it was never even used."

"It was used," said Dumarest. "Look at the wear."

"Marginal."

"And the condition."

"To be expected after such storage. But a little paint and a weld or two and it will be as good as new. A bargain for a shrewd investor. Now, Earl, if you'll come back to my office we can discuss terms. You wished outright purchase or to hire? If you want to hire you must accept the equipment in the condition you see it." He moved the light so as to illuminate Dumarest's face. "No?"

"No."

"Then what do you suggest?"

"Standing here the machine is useless. If you loan it to us we can get it working and open new tunnels to find the juscar."

"Loan?"

"What can you lose? At the worst you will have an operating machine instead of a piece of junk. And, once we find the juscar, your commission—need I go on?"

"No," said the agent. "Another gamble. You know, Earl, you're giving me reason never to forget you."

Chapter ELEVEN

"Watch!" Sven Axilia held a bowl of oil in which floated a burning wick. Gently he set it down on the floor of the tunnel and retreated to stand beside Dumarest. "Watch," he said again.

The tunnel was dark, external noises muffled by turns and distance, the tiny point of light throwing a clear, steady glow. Too steady as Dumarest knew.

"No drafts," he said.

"Which means no ventilation." Axilia kicked at the side of the tunnel. "Damned fools! They took out four times as much dirt as is necessary and forgot that men have to breathe. No shoring, either, you spotted that? The engineer must have been doped or stupid. See how the shaft widens then suddenly contracts?"

Dumarest followed the movements of the miner's hand. "Impatience," he said. "They were in a hurry to find the juscar."

"And maybe died doing it." Axilia moved on down the shaft to halt where it contracted into a bore barely a yard wide. Beyond lay darkness and loose debris. "Some of them could still be in there." He looked at the bowl of oil, now guttering. "Let's get out of here."

The mouth of the shaft lay to one side of the present field of operations, the edges eroded, rounded, and dotted with sparse vegetation. The ground was rutted and Axilia stooped to examine it, rising to let dust plume from between his fingers. Turning he scowled back into the tunnel, lifting his head to stare at the summit of the hills,

121

guessing, Dumarest knew, the weight and mass of the material above the opening.

"It's solid, Sven. It should take a wide shaft."

"An even one, maybe, but you saw what it was like in there. Irregular as hell. Drive a shaft like that and you're begging for trouble. The wide spaces set up stress regions and when you narrow the bore you create a destructive pattern. If you're lucky you can get away with it but if anything should happen, a tremor or a quake, it can't hold. Even a bad storm could do it or the vibrations set up by blasting too close." He dusted his hands. "All we can do with this is to forget it."

The old, original shaft now long abandoned, but the ones dug by the Boulayes were little better. Axilia had made his examination and was now illustrating the problem as he saw it.

"They ran wild," he said. "The man—Rudi?—had no real experience. Maybe he'd read a few books or something."

"He taught geology," said Dumarest.

"So he knew about rocks and strata and formations and expected mineral content and all the rest of it. But mining? I'd guess you've had more experience than he did. He worked on theory and that can be fatal."

It had been fatal but Dumarest made no comment. It was better to let the man work in his own way and already he'd displayed knowledge and skill beyond that of an average miner. He must have been a shift boss at least, or an engineer.

Now he said, "The shaft they're working now is a bust. It must cut across the perimeter of the main deposit but that doesn't tell us in which direction to head. I want to drive bores to the west and south at descent angles of thirty and forty degrees so as to check the concentration of jascar. If the findings are positive we can expand and divert as necessary."

Wormholes bored into fruit to find the succulent seed at the heart. But Dumarest was interested in more than the juscar.

"What about the shaft where Rudi is buried?"

"Over here." Axilia led the way toward it, halting on a mound so as to point. "There isn't much to see."

A shallow gully now filled at one end with a slope of detritus. A wide depression above it flattening into the upper reaches of the hills. Some vegetation, a few scattered rocks, a glitter of powdered manna. Rudi's grave.

"He'll be far back," said Axilia. "Buried deep in the hill. The fall must have progressed to the mouth or maybe she instigated it. She took a nugget from his hand, you say?"

"That's what she told me."

"Then she was damned lucky not to have been caught. Once this stuff goes it runs all the way. Of course there could have been shoring which she jerked free afterwards."

To bury the man or to hide the evidence of possible violence; Dumarest knew what the man was thinking. How often had he known it to happen before? An unwanted partner neatly disposed of—but what reason could Isobel have had for wanting to kill?

He said, "She wanted to bury him. To save him from scavengers. Now she wants to take him back to his home world."

"Some bones? A few scraps of clothing? You know what he must be like now, Earl."

"It's her mine, Sven, and it's a part of the deal."

Dumarest moved on and jumped to stand on the slope. Dirt shifted from beneath his boots, the gouge he made filling even as he raked the surface with his heel. A dozen men with shovels could labor for a month and make little impression on the loose material.

Watching Axilia said, "You won't hold the men unless they find juscar."

And there would be none where he was standing. Dumarest turned, looking at the hills, trying to judge the direction of the collapsed tunnel. It was impossible to determine with any real accuracy and it was more than just direction; he needed to know the angle of descent, any turns it had made, alterations in level.

And exactly how far Rudi had been from the mouth when he'd died. Information only Isobel could give.

She arrived at dusk with Zalman and the final part of the dismantled machine. Tocsaw was with them and he smiled as Dumarest helped unload the vehicle.

"Surprised to see me?"

"Pleased. The others?"

"Fitz was interested and Jon could be pursuaded." He dismissed them with a gesture. "Is this where you want to set up the machine?"

He got to work at Dumarest's nod, Zalman helping, Axilia using his brawn while Chell adjusted the lights so as to lengthen the day. The local looked sullen, restless, and Dumarest guessed he would be off at the first opportunity.

Isobel nodded agreement when he mentioned it. "I'll immobilize the raft, Earl, so if he wants to leave he'll have to walk."

"Did you manage to find more labor?"

"Not as yet but Mtouba told me some of the men you specified had been trying to sell him manna. He also mentioned how much he'd lost by refusing to buy it."

"Anything else?"

"Such as?" Her eyes searched his face. "A ship? You hope for a ship to arrive?"

"He didn't know he had the tunneler," said Dumarest. "Or he said he didn't know. There could be other things which had slipped his memory. Explosives, for example, mining lasers, equipment we could use. When you go into town tomorrow ask if he has anything to freeze loose dirt." He saw her frown and explained, "Miners use it when dealing with moist sand and fine loams. Stuff which runs like water when you dig a hole. They freeze it with certain gases and cut into it like cake. Sven will give you the technical details."

"Can't you?"

"Sven is the expert around here. I know such gases are used but I don't know which would be the best for any particular situation."

"And you want to leave the man his pride, is that it?" She smiled as he didn't answer. "Earl?"

"I need his muscle." Dumarest was blunt. "I need his skill. I want him to be on my side. Have you made arrangements for the men to be fed?"

"Yes. They can come back to the house and—"

"No. Send the food out here."

"Beds too?" She was joking but became serious when she saw his expression. "You mean you want them to work all night?"

"They have lights," he reminded. "And they've been idle long enough. The quicker we get that machine working the sooner we can find the juscar." The metal and the dead man and the secret buried with him. "Now let's get back to the house. I need to study the drawings."

He studied them after a meal of tisane, cold pudding, and a loaf made of reconstituted meats and vegetables. Quick, easily prepared fare which she sent out to the workers before coming into the chamber to stand at his shoulder.

He said, "I have all the plans, Isobel? You haven't forgotten any?"

"No, Earl, you have them all."

Zalman could have told if she was lying but Dumarest was convinced she told the truth. The drawings were those he had studied before but now he went over them again with greater care. Rudi had not been a draftsman but, as a geologist, he'd had experience on field trips and knew the importance of careful notation. But his three-dimensional depiction had been poor.

Dumarest frowned at one of the sheets. The lower levels? The upper? Did that shaft connect with another or did it just end in a blank wall? Which lines denoted ventilation? Blue flecks told of discovered nuggets of juscar but they were too evenly distributed to signal the position of the nexus. A maze in which he wandered to determine a single point.

"Here?" His finger rested on the sheet. "Was it here?"

"Earl, I can't be sure." There was no need to ask what

he meant. "It was getting dark, I was confused—how can I be certain?"

"Try!"

"It was a long time ago now."

"Try!"

The lash of his voice was a whip which she obeyed. How had it been? How, exactly, had it been? Closing her eyes she again visualized the scene, every detail of the event. They had been outside and Rudi had been impatient to get to work. He had gone ahead and she, finally, had followed to hear the scream, the crash, to see the face, the half-buried body, the extended hand . . . the hand . . . the hand. . . .

"Isobel!" Dumarest had risen and was facing her, hands gripping her shoulders, eyes hard as they met her own. "Get hold of yourself, woman!"

Had she been screaming? Crying? Shaking and acting the child?

"Here!" He handed her wine. "Drink this and calm down." More gently he added, "It happened a long time ago, my dear. A long time ago."

Too long and time had dulled the memory. Or was it something else?

Did she now want to remember?

Slowly she drank the wine, thinking, masking her thoughts in simple actions as she had so often done when Rudi had been so insistent. A trick to extend the seconds and gain time in order to compose herself. To recognize the problem she faced.

To find the body was to lose Dumarest.

Knowing that could she help him to find it?

"Isobel?" His eyes were anxious. "Do you feel better now?"

Had he guessed? It must surely be no secret to him how she felt; a woman in love betrayed herself every moment. Would he know if she lied? Could she bear to face him if she did?

"Isobel?"

"Nothing." She forced herself to smile, to shake her head as she set down the empty goblet. "I was thinking, remembering. Rudi was far down the shaft—no, the cutting leading to the shaft. He was within the tunnel, of course, but even though it was getting late the light showed him clearly. I can see his face now, all warm and smiling as if he were relishing the sight of a fire. He had his hand extended and was about to say something when it happened."

"The collapse?"

"There was no warning, Earl. None at all. One second he was standing there looking at me, the next he was down and dust was everywhere and I heard the scream. One scream and then nothing. No sound at all at first then only the rustle of falling dirt. I'd run forward and was touching him, holding his hand. It held that nugget and I must have taken it."

"And then?"

She shook her head and he didn't press. Dazed, shocked, deafened, stunned by the sudden catastrophe— how could she be expected to recall every small detail? She must have run, driven by instinct if nothing else, sensing danger as an animal would sense a waiting trap. An instinct which had saved her life as it had so often saved his own.

Again he studied the map, remembering the gully he had seen. The cutting must have been filled and the shaft driven toward the east—if Rudi's face had been illuminated by the setting sun it had to be that way. The angle? Shallow, he guessed, if sharp the rays of sunlight wouldn't have penetrated. Had the gulley faced directly toward the west? If not the deviation would give an angle to work on once he had established the exact time of year and position of the sun. But now, perhaps, he could establish how far back the man had been.

"Isobel?" He touched the map as he gained her attention. "Just where was Rudi standing? Can you remember?"

She stooped over him, the soft mound of her left breast touching his cheek. An accident, maybe, but the contact lingered and he could smell the perfume she wore, a scent accentuated by the febrile heat of her body.

"Here, I think—no, here!" She placed her finger beside his own. "There was a place where we'd hung a lantern and he was standing just behind it." A memory she no longer wished to entertain. As Dumarest marked the spot she said, "Earl, I need some air. Let's go up to the roof."

There was wind, a thin breeze coming from the sea which caught her hair and sent it to lie in a delicate tracery over her face as it pressed the thin fabric of her clothing against the contours of her body. Starlight painted the area a ghostly white, small gleams reflected from her nails as she neatened her hair, others finding life in the deep wells of her eyes.

"Isn't it beautiful, Earl? I love the night. It takes away all the dirt and ugliness and replaces it with mystery and enchantment. Rudi and I used to come up here often when he was alive. We'd sit and talk and all our worries seemed to vanish. It was just as if we'd taken manna. Nothing mattered. Everything was wonderful. I never thought I'd ever feel that way again."

He said nothing, looking toward the hills, the distant glow of light.

"You probably feel you should be there with them," she said. "I'm glad you're not."

"Sven has had experience with mining machinery and Miles is an engineer. Hans and your man Gheel can do the moving and holding. If I was there I'd only be in the way."

"And you had other things to do." Taking his hand she led the way to a seat. "You're clever, Earl. Not many men would be willing to let others take the lead. Even Rudi used to thrust himself forward more than he should have done. It made him unpopular at the university. People like to be made to feel important."

"Perhaps they were envious."

"Of me?" Her soft laughter showed she appreciated the compliment. "Don't underestimate the viciousness of academics, Earl. Your average professor can be more spiteful than a betrayed woman. Haven't you found that those who live the most restricted lives are often the most intolerant? And few lives are as restricted as that of those who teach."

"What did you do before you married?"

"Do you really care, Earl? I studied, taught a little, took a position as assessor for a company making geological surveys. I even traveled a little." She moved closer to him, leaning back in order to look at the sky, the stars hanging like jewels in the heavens. "Just a little, Earl, and always to safe, civilized worlds. You would have been bored."

Her shoulder was against his own, her profile sharp against the starlight, the smooth mounds of her breasts enhanced by the wind-tautened fabric. The long, smooth curves of her thighs were parted, the material of her gown forming a concavity between them; a cradle in which she rested her hands.

"Bored," she said again. "Sometimes I think it to be the worst condition of all. To wake knowing what every hour will bring, every minute predicted, each second alloted its special task. To see nothing ahead but endless repetition of the familiar."

"To eat," he said. "To know that you will not be hungry. To know that you will sleep in comfort and safety. To be certain that, for you, there will be a tomorrow. Many would yearn for such a condition."

"But not you, Earl." She turned to face him, one hand lifting to rest on his arm. "Never you." A creature of the wild, she thought as she studied his face. The most dangerous creature of all. A man who had early learned to live without any protection other than that given by his own prowess. A fighter, one not afraid to kill, one never afraid to plunge into the unknown. Against him Rudi seemed a petulant child. Had he been alive now which would she have chosen?

Dumarest looked at the hand which she had closed tightly on his arm. "Worried?"

"A little." It was a relief to change the subject. "Debts, commitments, the usual thing. God, how at times I wish I could forget the whole damned mess. Tell Mtouba to take all I own and just live life as most do on this world."

He said, bluntly. "If it was in your nature to do that you'd have done it long ago. No, Isobel, you're a fighter. You don't give in."

"Rudi used to say that in any enterprise there was a point where a wise man accepted his limitations."

"The justification of failure."

"No, Earl! Rudi—"

"Is dead." He was curt in his interruption. "That very fact stamps him as a failure."

"You are cruel to say that. It was an accident."

"One he could have avoided and should have done. One born of ignorance. What did he know of mining aside from what books had told him? The tunnel was too large, there should have been shoring, he should have tested the soil to discover the coefficient of adhesion." Things he had failed to do and so had died and was buried—why had he worn the medallion? Recognizing the cause of his anger Dumarest said, more gently, "I'm sorry. I should not have said that."

"It's true. I tried to warn him but he wouldn't listen." She added, "It means a lot to you, doesn't it? Finding the medallion, I mean."

"Yes."

"And when you find it? If you find it?" She knew the answer. "You'll move on. But if you find this world, Earl, what then?"

A question he'd been asked before and now, as then, had no answer. The search had taken too long, the disappointments had been too many, the driving need to find the planet obliterating all other considerations. To find Earth. To *find* it—beyond that nothing existed.

And it was there, somewhere among the stars, waiting for him once he had gained the secret lying so close.

The wind freshened and Isobel shivered a little, pressing closer to gain warmth and shelter. The stars were fuzzed now, their brightness dulled with scudding wisps of cloud.

"It'll rain soon. Tomorrow, maybe."

"Will it be bad?" It would be the first rain he'd seen on this world.

"No, it's too early in the year for that. Just showers but they'll delay the ephemerae—their pods can't swell when it's wet. Later, when warmed by the sun, the air will be full of color."

Devils dancing in their changing patterns but this time she wouldn't be watching them. Tomorrow they would all be at the mine and Dumarest too busy to pay her any attention. Tomorrow—but tonight he would be hers.

...heater. With a swift jerk having cut a finger of ice
...pped it into a pouch before making the report.

...How deep is it now, Paula? Zalman was anxious...

Chapter TWELVE

———◆◉◆———

From the headphones Zalman's voice said, "One fifty,
Earl."

"Right."

A routine report which required only a brief ac-
knowledgment and Dumarest had no breath to spare for
unnecessary conversation. Fifty yards on the surface could
be covered in as many strides but the same distance below
ground was another matter. A span measured in feet as
progress was measured in inches.

Dumarest drew up his knees and used foot and elbows
to lever himself farther along the bore. It stretched before
him, a circular hole barely a yard in diameter, the sides
roughly combed by the teeth which had torn it from the
rock. A shaft without ventilation; the air he breathed
came from tanks fastened to his back and fed into a mask
which covered his face. Condensed sweat made pools at
neck and chin, more stinging his eyes. Beneath the padding and his own clothing his body was slimed with mois-
ture.

"Two seventy, Earl."

"Right."

The beam of his helmet lantern bobbed as he inched
on, hitting the sides of the bore, deflected from a point
farther down. The shaft which should have been straight
was curved, irregular, the cutters diverted by altered densities and a malfunctioning guidance system. Even so it
ran in the desired direction.

Dumarest halted as the beam showed what he was

132

looking for. With a small pick he dug out a nugget of jus-car and slipped it into a pouch before making his report.

"Hit."

"Good! How does it look, Earl?" Zalman was optimistic. He sobered as Dumarest told him. "Bad color, eh? Well, maybe it'll increase as you move on."

A forlorn hope. The juscar was scattered and it was possible to drive a shaft through it and not find a single nugget. So far he'd been lucky and from his finds and their proximity a vector could be drawn on the map of probable dispersement. Axilia's method and a good one.

"Four seventy, Earl."

"Right."

Zalman had sounded worried and with reason. The rock was soft, the bore deep and if anything happened Dumarest was as good as dead. A risk he had taken but one which no man in his right mind could like. Again he halted to gouge free another nugget. A small one, the blue barely noticeable in the beam of his lantern, its finding a matter of chance.

As it came free the bore trembled.

Dumarest felt it, instinctively crouching, eyes wide behind the mask, his muscles tensed to fight an enemy he couldn't see. One he had no hope of defeating. Again he felt the slight tremor and a thin plume of dust fell from the roof of the shaft to rain on his helmet. A shift of some tectonic plate, the crashing impact of storm-driven waves on some distant coast—the cause was unimportant. If the bore collapsed he would be buried to lie, still living, in a nighted tomb.

"Earl?" The voice riding the wire attached to the lifeline was strained. "You've gone deep enough, man. We only bored down to seven hundred and you're past the six-fifty mark now. Up?"

"Up," said Dumarest. "Up!"

He felt the movement of slack at his side then the pull at the yoke attached to his ankles. A pull which straightened the rope and closed his legs. Beneath him the floor of the shaft began to slide under the padding, the circle illuminated by his lantern to diminish with slow deliberation. As he watched more dust fell to thicken the air.

"Hurry!"

"Earl?"

"Hurry, damn you! Hurry!"

Rock fell as the pull at the rope increased, small fragments which heaped into a pile, others which, with startling abruptness, filled the bore where he had been lying. Beneath him the dirt rasped against the padding, his knees, the toes of his boots. He lifted them, fighting the pull, accepting the strain on calves and thighs in order to avoid any impact with an obstruction or uneven spot in the bore.

"Earl!" Zalman knelt beside him as Dumarest left the mouth of the shaft. "Are you hurt?"

"No." Dumarest removed the helmet and mask. "A bruise or two but that's all. You logged the finds?" He smiled as Zalman nodded. "You did well, Hans. Thanks."

"We're partners, Earl. I haven't forgotten."

A reminder of a bargain yet to be completed but Dumarest doubted if it was only that. Freed of the tanks and padding he laved his face and head in a bucket, rising to dry himself, seeing Zalman rewind the rope on its drum, the activity all around.

Ten days had made a change. Where there had been only the gaping mouths of decaying shafts and the camp where men stayed if they wanted and worked if they chose was ordered confusion. The place was littered with fresh mounds of debris gouged from the rock; the detritus forming a bizarre pattern against the hills. An awning shielded a table at which the workers ate, tents provided accommodation, a trough held water for washing. Latrines had been dug well away from the field kitchen with its pots and oil-fed fires. To one side the tunneler dominated the scene, the sound of its engine a thin, spiteful whine. From the bore it had made came a constant stream of gritty particles which were gathered and dumped by a suction tube handled by a pair of men.

Axilia looked up as Dumarest approached. "Any luck?"

"Some—but not what we wanted."

"Trouble?"

"That too—the bore fell in." Dumarest looked at the tuneller. "Has that been going all the time?"

"No. The engine broke down and it took time to fix." Axilia narrowed his eyes. "You think it vibrated the strata and brought down the roof?"

"It could have. From now on there's to be a halt on working while anyone's in a bore." Dumarest looked at Tocsaw. The man was sweating, dust plastering his face and naked torso to give him the appearance of a living statue. "He's standing up well."

"More than you can say about the others." Axilia glowered to where Ocher and Quail sat at the table beneath the awning. They and others had come to join the workers but already some had left and Dumarest knew that others would follow.

He said, "I'll check out the findings with you later, Sven. Now I could use something to drink."

A slack-faced girl served him, spilling half the tisane as she filled his cup. A lump of bread followed and he took both over to the table. The awning provided an acoustic relay and, leaning back, he could hear what Quail was saying.

". . . crazy. That bastard will kill us all if we give him the chance. It's all right for Sven, he likes mining, to him all this is a game, but what are we getting out of it? Work, bad food, more work. Hell, I didn't come to Elysius for this."

"We offered—"

"Sure we did. Do a little digging and get a share of the juscar. Get ourselves a stake if we want to move on. Real money for a High passage, maybe—man, we'll be lucky if we get enough to ride Low. You fancy that?"

Traveling doped, frozen, and ninety per cent dead. Riding in caskets meant for the transportation of beasts and risking the fifteen percent death rate for the sake of cheap transportation.

Ocher shook his head. "I've done that too often. Once
more could be one time too many."

"That's right." Quail took a sip of his tisane and spat it
into the dust. "Swill! We work like dogs and we don't
even get wine. To hell with it. There's color in the north
and the manna will be lying thick. How about us harvesting it while we have the chance?"

"What's the point? The Hausi won't buy."

"Because he's got a cut coming from the mine, but he'll
change his mind once we have the monopoly. See what I
mean? We harvest and store and use a little muscle if we
have to to make sure we get it all. Who can stop us?" His
laughter was ugly. "Man, we've got it made. All we need
do is collect."

An entrepreneur recognizing an opportunity but also a
man whose labor Dumarest needed. Rising he stood before them both.

"Earl?" Ocher looked up, squinting. "How did it go?"

"Fair enough."

"Hit the nexus yet?" Quail added, "Don't bother to answer. You didn't. I can read it in your face."

"As I can read what you have in mind in yours."
Dumarest looked at the disorder of the mine, the hills, the
sky to the north. "There are easier ways of making a living, right?" As Quail nodded he said, "Harvesting the
manna, for example. I've thought about it but I've recognized the snags. First, the Hausi won't pay high—why
should he when so many are offering it cheap? Then you
have to go out and get it—not easy unless you've got a
raft. Humping that stuff in bulk means work and, of
course, you'd have to have containers and such. You'd
need money all along the line."

"For boxes," said Ocher thoughtfully. "And you'd need
supplies."

"Unless you want to live on the manna, yes. But once
you take it you won't want to go to all that trouble. And
if you're thinking of forcing others to work for you, forget
it. Remember the fight I had with Sven? How no one
tried to help the woman? She doesn't eat manna, that's
why. If she'd been one of them they would all have

jumped in to help her and Sven would be dead by now."
He added, casually, "Don't take my word for it, ask
Mtouba. Or try it the hard way."

Quail said, "Those dummies won't hurt us."

"Maybe not."

"They haven't the guts."

"Then you've got nothing to worry about." Dumarest
finished his tisane. "But if you try to steal the raft you'll
have plenty. The same if you take anything else. Leave if
you want but, when you go, you go empty handed." He
looked from one to the other. "Do I make myself clear?"

Dusk brought the time for decisions. Seated at the table
Axilia swept a hand over the map before him, a finger
tracing a straight line.

"The bore you checked, Earl. I've correlated the findings and it's a bust. Decent color but not enough and
fading instead of thickening. My guess is we cut across
the perimeter." His hand moved, the finger tracing another line. "As we did here."

Tocsaw said, "Trace two lines within a circle, bisect the
angle where they join and a line from there will aim
toward the center."

"And away from it."

"That would lead up into the open air." The engineer
wiped a hand over his face, the palm smearing oil to be
a wider blotch. "Let's not play games, Sven."

"We're talking of a sphere not a circle," reminded
Dumarest. "Eliminate the upper half and we've still got a
wide choice of direction."

One they had tried to narrow with the bores, the extensions of old workings. Computations backed by the
miner's instinct and knowledge but they all knew success
rested on luck as much as anything else. And time was
running out.

"The men are restless," said Zalman. "Most of them
are ready to quit."

"Quail and Ocher?"

"Those too, Earl, but they can be handled. Give them
a few nuggets and they'll be greedy for more. No, it's the

others who are the real problem. Their patience is running out and a few of them have tried to steal." Part of his duties was to check them from the workings, taking what they had found, reading in their attitudes and answers if they were holding out. He added, bleakly, "They keep staring at the color in the sky."

"If they want to leave we can't hold them." Dumarest turned to the woman. "Any luck with Mtouba?"

"He's given all the credit he can," she said. "Or that's what he says. From now on we pay for what we get and, if we take too long delivering some metal, he'll close us down."

Axilia said, "Maybe he won't find that too easy."

"All he has to do is wait," said Dumarest. "We need supplies which he needn't deliver. The stuff we have now he doesn't want returned but he could come to collect the tunneler if he wants."

"He's welcome to it." Tocsaw wiped again at his face. "The damned thing's a heap of junk."

An exaggeration but the machine kept breaking down due to faulty repairs and previous abuse. Dumarest looked at where it rested on the slope almost hidden by its own mounds of crushed rock. Only the drive was visible, the cutting head was far below the surface, and even as he watched a man working on the engine swore and jumped back from a vivid flare of bluish light.

"Mitel," said Tocsaw. "He's willing enough but a dope. I told him to check all the insulation and you saw what happened. Well, I'd better get over there and see what I can do."

"Not yet." Dumarest looked at the map. "How far down is the bore?" He nodded at the answer. "Still a way to go yet. Can you steepen the angle?"

"It's perpendicular now." Axilia gave the answer. "A chance we have to take, Earl. I gave orders for a direct shaft to run from here," he tapped at the map, "to here. Once we check it we'll have another vector to plot the nexus-line. We might even be lucky and hit the main deposit."

Or they could just be wasting more time. Dumarest

looked at the map as he had done a hundred times before trying to read into the lines and details more than they showed. The juscar was there—the nuggets proved it, but in which direction lay the main concentration? Bury a ball under the sand, stick a needle into the dirt while blind-folded and how often must you try before hitting dead center?

Zalman, reading him, said, "Is it possible, Earl?"

"What?" Axilia looked from one to the other, frown-ing. "What's possible? What are you talking about?"

"We're assuming the nexus must be under the hills toward the west," said Dumarest. "Maybe we're trying too far west. Could it lie toward the east?"

"It's barely possible," admitted the miner. "But if it does it's a freak."

"But possible?"

"Yes."

Isobel said, "What's on your mind, Earl? What made you think of that?"

"Rudi." He turned to meet her eyes. "You said he was smiling as he waited for you. He'd gone ahead and had turned and was holding out his hand as if to give you something."

"The nugget. It was in his hand."

"Perhaps it could have been more. He could have planned a surprise of some kind." Pausing he said, quietly, "What if he'd found the nexus?"

"Rudi? But that's impossible! He would have told me!"

"He could have been about to when the roof caved in. Why else should he have wanted to hand you a nugget? A find, yes, but what was so special about that? And he was impatient, remember?"

Too impatient, running ahead, irritated at her tardiness as if he were a small boy eager to display his prize. But if he had found it—if, after all that time he had finally found it—God, why was fate so cruel?

She said, dully, "No. It isn't possible. He hadn't found it. He would have told me and he'd said nothing."

For reasons she hadn't mentioned, perhaps. A quarrel, sexual tensions unresolved and corroding their relationship, a clash of personalities, a desire to prove himself or to avoid more of her recriminations at his continued failure. Dumarest glanced at Zalman, seeing the man shrug. Whatever the truth she had buried it so deep as to make it impossible to read.

Axilia said, "It's a guess, Earl, nothing more. You could even be right but what difference does it make? We can't open up the gully and there's no way of telling where he found the nexus if he found it at all. He'd probably planted the nugget near the entrance or had it with him all the time. We've got to operate on a plan—it's no good just to run wild. You'd better get back to the tunneler, Miles."

Tocsaw rose from his chair. "The same direction?"

"Yes." The miner looked at Dumarest. "You agree, Earl?" The bore was nearing completion and to change things now would be to waste previous effort as well as to create discord. Axilia relaxed as he nodded. "Good. That's settled. I'll just take a look around then get some sleep." He yawned, it had been a hard day. "A few hours'll do it then I'll get back to work."

As he left the table Isobel said, "And you, Earl? Are you coming back to the house?"

"No."

"Why not? You could use a bath and a decent bed for a change. Some decent food, too." She recognized the fact that she was pleading and tried logic instead. "It will be the first time since the tunneler arrived. You can't push yourself like a machine."

And he couldn't afford to live soft while others lived hard or be absent when he should be on watch. Things which, woman-like, she hadn't thought important. She frowned as he explained.

"I don't see that, Earl. Why should they resent you coming back to the house?"

"Because they are human. Because they would hate to think they are being exploited. We're operating on shares and when one slacks the rest suffer."

"And I've been slacking."

"You own the mine."

"Which makes no difference, Earl. Tomorrow I'll get to work with the rest."

Fifteen hours later the bore was complete and Dumarest listened to Zalman's drone as he relayed the depth to Axilia now over two hundred feet below the surface. Beside him Tocsaw hawked and rasped his boot over the dirt mounded all around.

"A bitch," he said. "That bore's got more twists than a corkscrew. Sven's idea; he wanted to get down fast but we hit high-density rock and the cutters veered. Well, maybe he'll be lucky."

Dumarest nodded looking at the area around the shaft. The heaped grit should have been sieved to reclaim any nuggets, their density telling the richness of the strata at various depths, but they lacked the necessary equipment. They lacked ventilation blowers, correct lighting, proper shoring, fundamental communications. The workings were a hazard in every conceivable respect—a gamble for desperate men.

"Two ninety, Sven." Zalman nodded at the response. "How's the going?"

Dumarest knew the answer. The shaft, twisting, dropping in a near perpendicular fall to level and turn, provided a three-dimensional nightmare. Axilia was covering it as fast as he could, taking sights rather than samples, checking color and not halting to dig out nuggets. If the nexus was found the little lost would count for nothing; if the shaft had been wrongly aimed the gain would be small.

Tocsaw said, "I'd better check the engine. The chances are we're going to need another bore."

"Will it stand up to it?"

"With extra cutters and souped-up gearing it might. I'll get to work on it right away."

"No vibration," said Dumarest. "Don't make any tests."

"I know that, Earl. You think I'm stupid or something?" The engineer shrugged. "Sorry, you were just reminding me. Guess I'm too tired to think straight."

"Then get some rest and tackle the engine afterward. Who knows? We may have hit lucky."

A hope Dumarest didn't share. As the engineer moved off to the tents he walked over the site. It was oddly deserted, the tents silent, the awning over the table shielding nothing but the benches and board. Three men had vanished during the night, slipping away, drawn by the color in the sky. Now, with Quail and Ocher, only two remained and he guessed they wouldn't stay for long.

"Earl!" Isobel came toward him. She wore thick miner's clothing and a helmet covered the natural tone of her hair. Dust soiled her cheeks and marred the beauty of her lips. "Looking for me?"

"No, just checking. Anyone in the shafts?"

"Not that I know of. Not in the old one and not in number two or three. I've just come from there."

"Seen Quail? Ocher?"

"Early this morning. They wanted some charges and—" she broke off at his expression. "Something wrong?"

"They asked for explosives? You handed them out?"

"They said you'd sent them to collect." She guessed his concern. "You didn't. Then—Earl!"

He was already running, heading toward the mouth of shaft number four. The blast came as he reached the entrance.

It was deep, rumbling, like the impact of a fist on a mighty gong. A roar followed by a gust of heat and a roiling flurry of dusty sand. A fog which drove into his eyes and nose and filled his mouth and lungs with stinging acridity.

"Earl!" Isobel had joined him. "Here!"

Dumarest donned the mask she handed to him and plunged into the tunnel. The fog was thicker inside, dirt piled in soft heaps on the floor, a golden glitter in the far gloom where a lantern still burned. He reached it, passed it and heard the cry from beyond.

"My leg! Dear God, my leg!"

Ocher was lying on his left side, he left leg buried to the knee beneath a heap of shattered stone. He coughed as Dumarest reached him, staring with wide, shocked eyes. Saliva dribbled from his open mouth to make tracks on the dust covering his chin.

"Earl?" He lifted a hand as Dumarest knelt beside him. "That you, Earl?"

"Yes." Dumarest stripped off the mask. "What happened?"

"Quail had an idea. He wanted to raid the shafts, grab what we could find then move out. He figured to bring down the face with set charges. I guess he must have used too much."

"Was he alone?"

"Yes." Ocher made a weak gesture. "He found a place to stay but I was heading toward the open. My leg! God, my leg!"

"How far down was he?"

"Quail? At the face. Help me, Earl." His voice rose as Dumarest rose. "You can't leave me here like this!"

His voice dulled as Dumarest moved down the shaft. The dust was thicker and he replaced the mask, the beam from his lantern showing barely a few feet ahead. A glow which showed an outflung arm, a hand curled as if to grab a departing life. The slab which had crushed Quail had spared his face and in death it wore a mocking smile.

Beyond him lay nothing but dust and emptiness.

"Earl!" Ocher reared as Dumarest returned. "Help me!"

Dumarest examined the rock trapping the limb. It was loose and would cascade if he tried to clear it. Ocher groaned as he gripped him by the shoulders and lifted them from the floor.

"We'll act together," said Dumarest. "Kick with your right foot. Use it as a lever to drag yourself clear. Now!" He grunted as, heaving, he fought to free the trapped leg. "Help me, damn you!"

A moment then Ocher screamed from the pain of his trapped leg. "I can't! It hurts! God, it hurts!"

"Listen!" Dumarest lifted the mask so the man could

see his face, his eyes. "This is your last chance. We get that leg clear or I'll have to amputate. Understand?"

"You'd cut—"

"That or leave you. The roof could go any second. It's your life, man. Now, move!"

Again he heaved, Ocher thrusting with his right foot, screaming as, slowly at first then with a rush his trapped leg came clear. Rocks cascaded after them as Dumarest dragged the man to the open air. A local fall, the roof stayed firm, but one which followed and surrounded them with a cloud of dust. When it settled Dumarest learned that Axilia was trapped.

Chapter THIRTEEN

The mouth of the bore was silent, the air holding a peculiar stillness as if in reaction from the recent violence, the people standing about forming a tableau which seemed frozen in time. Dumarest saw the drum, the rope, the glint of the wire attached to it which was now the only connection between them and the scrap of living tissue now entombed over five hundred feet below the surface.

To Tocsaw he said, "There's no doubt as to the extent of the blockage?"

"None."

"No chance of cutting around it?"

"No. The jar of the explosion brought down the roof for most of the distance. It starts fifty feet from the mouth and my guess is it fills the bore up to where Sven is trapped five hundred and thirty-seven feet down. The rope's caught. We can talk to him but we can't pull him up."

Isobel said, dully, "It's all my fault. If I hadn't been so stupid as to hand out those charges this would never have happened."

"Those bastards!" Zalman was bitter. "At least one of them is dead."

And the other suffering but it made no difference to the man locked in a living tomb. For him time was running out, measured by the air in his tanks, reduced with each breath as the mounting heat gave him a foretaste of hell.

"There's nothing we can do," said Tocsaw. "It would

have been better had he been crushed. This way we've either got to ignore him or listen to him die."

"Maybe not," said Dumarest. He had been thinking, remembering. A place of dust and emptiness where surely there should have been rock. "Hans, you talked Sven down, I want a diagram of the exact path of the bore— and I mean exact. Miles, get your maps and join me in number four."

It was as he had left it, the dust settled now, the shaft an irregular hole punched deep into the flank of the hill. One which wended and dipped to form pockets in which gases could collect; carbon dioxide, methane, some ammonia, traces of mineral vapors, an acrid blend which clogged lungs and could kill the unwary. Now all were overlaid by the sharp tang of the recent explosion.

In the beam of a lantern Dumarest looked at the body of Quail.

The man was still smiling in the frozen rictus of death, his hand still clenched as if to follow the pattern of his life. A hand which pointed toward the face he had attacked, the wall of rock now shattered and fallen to reveal the natural fissure beyond.

"A cave!" Isobel echoed her incredulity. "But a cave in this formation is impossible!"

"A fissure," corrected Dumarest. "A crack. See?"

He moved the beam of his lantern to reveal close-set walls, a roof which fell to meet the rise of the narrow floor, the cracks which scarred the surface. A flaw in the rock caused by some age-old cataclysm, perhaps the same force which had given birth to the juscar, the stone cracked as if it were glass struck by a hammer.

"Miles?"

Tocsaw was at hand. He jumped into the fissure and quested along it like a dog following a scent, using maps and instruments to mark and determine direction and level. Crude tools but they would have to serve. Sonar devices would have been better and far more accurate but they were luxuries they didn't have.

"Well?"

"I don't know, Earl. I can't be sure." The engineer

studied his maps. "It looks as if this runs toward the bore but it's hard to be certain."

"Do your best," said Dumarest. It would be a mistake to push and so fluster the man. "But remember Sven's relying on us. We'll have to start in fifteen minutes at the most."

Time in which he assembled equipment and correlated Zalman's plotted path into the maps. Time in which he spoke to Axilia.

"Sven?"

He listened to silence.

"Sven!"

"What?" The sound of inhalation. "That you, Earl?" The voice was dull, listless. "I thought you'd all decided to forget me. Couldn't blame you if you had. I talked a man into dying once and would never willingly do it again. The poor bastard went crazy at the end and kept crying and pleading and there was damn all I could do. I was young then. Young. How long has it been?"

"Not long. We've had to check things out."

"Seems like eternity. Just lying in the silence, wondering if anyone was at the end of the line. I tried calling a few times but got no answer."

"We were busy."

"Sure."

"I'm here now, Sven. Someone will always be here."

"There's no need. I won't let it get too bad. A sharp edge, a vein—it'll soon be over."

"Cut that!" Dumarest made his voice sharp. "I'm coming to get you and I don't want to risk my life rescuing a corpse. If you want to die just give me the word and you'll save us all a lot of effort. Shall I tell Anna you lacked the guts to hold on when I kiss her?"

"You bastard!"

"Yes." Dumarest smiled his satisfaction, an angry man was one who wanted to survive. "Just be patient. How are you? What is your position? You free to move or what?"

"The line's caught and I'm at the end of it. There's maybe twenty feet clear behind me. If I uncouple I can move down to the end of the bore about fifty feet ahead.

Beyond that it's blocked. God knows what saved me from
being buried, a slab of rock, maybe, which acted as a
natural roof. What's your plan?"

"I'm hoping to cut a way to you from a fissure we
found. It was opened by the explosion. It'll take time so
don't be impatient."

"Should I start digging?"

"Not until I tell you." Dumarest paused then added,
"And, Sven—save your air."

The drill whined, slowed, whined again. In the beam of
the lantern dust rose to create thin, whirling plumes of
glittering but transitory splendor. A sight he had seen too
often and yet would have to see again. The bit vanished
into the rock, the chuck hitting, whirling as he reversed
the drive and withdrew the cutter. Carefully Dumarest
lifted an explosive charge from the sack behind him, inserted it into the hole, rammed it home then blocked the
opening with an expanding core.

"Sven?"

"Earl?"

"Yes. Firing. Listen for the sound."

Dumarest retreated, carrying tools and supplies with
him, adding them to those stacked back down the narrow
shaft he had cut at one end of the fissure. A rope from his
waist carried the wire attaching him electronically to the
trapped man. On the surface the others would be monitoring and relaying as they counted the minutes. If
Dumarest took too long he would find only a corpse in an
airless cavern.

The charge exploded as he triggered the detonator, expanding gases held, contained and directed to blast a
long, narrow opening in the rock. Rubble spilled from it
and had to be shoveled away. Dust plumed to fill the air
and could be ignored. Like an eel Dumarest wriggled his
way along the created opening as he saw another obstruction.

"Sven? Did you get it?"

"Just about, Earl. A rumble from my right and a little
low."

"A rumble?" Dumarest frowned. The sound should have been sharp and unmistakable if transmitted through solid rock. A gap of some kind must lie between them. If it was an air space created by another fissure he was in luck. If anything else, in trouble.

The drill whined again, the charge was set, detonated and again he thrust forward. A push and his hand thrust loose a slab of rock, his head followed, an arm bearing his lantern. In its beam he saw a shelf, a crack, a mass of splintered rock all precariously balanced. An oddity which nature had constructed, rains seeping to dissolve binding minerals, to erode away binding stone.

"Earl?" Axilia sounded worried. "Another rumble, louder but still not clear."

"Get your ear against the wall," said Dumarest. "I'm going to start tapping. When I'm loud and clear let me know."

Another voice, Isobel's, said, "Be careful, Earl. That fissure worried me. It could be this entire region is one of balanced instability. I've known such places before."

"This is one of them."

"Then—"

"I'm close to Sven. Clear the line."

Rubble fell as Dumarest eased himself through the opening. Behind him, attached by lines were his supplies and he drew them toward him: charges, extra tanks of air, water, tools, power packs—the equipment of an artificial mole. More rubble fell as he lifted them piece by piece to the far side of the area. The roof was so low in places that he had to drop onto his stomach and slide beneath the poised mass of ponderous weight.

At the far side he paused, sitting with his back against a rock shaped like a pear, the beam of his lantern moving from point to point.

There? The rock looked solid and should be able to take a small amount of vibration. There? He would have to drill and blast until he reached solid ground. There? The mistake could be fatal.

"Earl, I've been thinking." Sven sounded determined.

"That is crazy. I overheard. If the situation is what Isobel says then you haven't a hope of getting to me."

"Shut up!"

"What's that?"

"Close your mouth and use your ears!" Dumarest swung a short, heavy hammer against a rock. "Well?"

"Hard and clear." The miner's voice broke a little. "Man, you're close!"

Close enough to pin where the bore must be; a target three feet wide and about seventy long. Relatively a large area but there would be time for only one effort. His own tanks were low, Axilia's must be almost exhausted. The spares would give him a new lease on life but the miner needed to be reached before they could be used.

Again the drill whined and the whirling plumes danced as if made of sentient golden lace. Setting the charge was a gamble; one set against the balance of the rocks and played by his skill in judging force and direction and intensity. A gamble he lost.

"Earl!"

He heard the cry as the roof fell in behind him; Isobel sensing or feeling the sudden shift of weight. A cry drowned in the roar and rumble of cascading stone. Dust fogged the air as he crouched, unable to do more than hug the shelter he had picked out and pray that his guess had been correct. If the ledge fell he was dead. If it held he stood a chance. How small that chance was he saw when the collapse was complete.

"Sven?"

Nothing, his line was trapped, the wire broken, both parted under the edge of his knife. The way he had come was blocked, even if he could have clawed his way through the compact mass he had no idea of where the tunnel he had made was situated. All that was left was the opening ahead. That, two tanks of air, some tools, a few charges and a single canteen of water.

Resting his ear against the stone Dumarest used the hammer to pound a signaling beat.

One answered loud and clear.

A treble rap and Dumarest switched to a pick, using

the muscles of back and shoulders to drive the point into the rock, wrenching it free, driving it again, the short handled tool awkward in the cramped space. Using it in the way he'd learned when working as a miner on a far world, cutting his way through the soft strata, kicking debris behind him, breathing tanked air and thankful it wasn't dust. Driving through at last into the bore where Axilia was waiting, vomiting for want of air.

Isobel said, "Earl's alive! Thank God!"

"They're both alive and now on fresh tanks," said Zalman. "But that's the good news. The bad is that the route Earl took is blocked and he's as trapped as Sven was." He paused as Tocsaw waved. "Miles wants to talk to you."

He said, as she joined him, "It's Earl. He wants to ask you something. Here."

The instrument was warm against her cheek. "Darling?"

"You warned me about the region," said Dumarest. "You were right. Now our lives are in your hands. Did you plot my progress through the fissure to the bore? Good. What I want is for you to tell Tocsaw exactly where to bore so as to reach the point above the collapsed area. Do you understand what I mean?"

"I'm not sure." She fell silent, thinking. "Are you hoping the collapse has left a cavity?"

"Yes."

"You could be wrong, Earl."

"The rock fell. Something must have been left behind." She sensed his impatience and tried to imagine what it must be like down there; two men crouched in a narrow bore, air limited, heat mounting, pressures of more than one kind making themselves felt. "You studied geology, Isobel. Now use that education. You know the formation, what it's likely to do, how it will behave. Our only chance is to dig so as to meet the bore you cut. It'll have to be a short one."

"Earl! You're five hundred feet deep!"

"No, the bore was that long but it twisted. Our actual

depth is about three hundred from the surface. If we can climb up and there is a space there could be air. If you cut down into that space—put Tocsaw back on the line."

"No!" She smarted with the thought he regarded her as inadequate to make a judgment. "I know what to do."

"Put him back on anyway while you plot the line." Dumarest looked at Axilia in the light of a single lantern. "She'll do it," he assured. "If anyone knows the area she does and she'll be able to guide the cutter down through the fissure lines now she knows they're present. Miles? Use everything you've got to speed the bore. Loosen the top layer with explosives. Yes, yes I know the danger. Hell, man, how much time do you think we've got?" Dumarest looked at the miner. "We'll have to cut now. Anything you want to say? No. Here we go!" His knife slashed the rope and wire. "Now up and out!"

Axilia took the first turn, glad of the chance to stretch, strong with the euphoria of rescue. Even if he was to die it would no longer be alone and now, with the tools Dumarest had carried, he would have a chance. Rock crumbled and fell to be spread in the bore as, like a worm, he drove upward and to one side on a slanting path to the east.

When he flagged Dumarest spelled him, extending the shaft, cutting around a stubborn mass, delving always into the softest strata. Twice they retreated while the charges blasted a quick extension, taking chances for the sake of speed. To find the opening which logically had to be present, to gain its relative comfort and security, the air which could have seeped in via radiating cracks.

"Earl!" Axilia, in the lead, halted. "There's a fissure running across up here. Left or right?"

"Left."

They mounted into a gallery less than shoulder wide to shuffle along it until stopped by a blank wall, to retrace their steps and find the walls closing in to a space of inches.

"Up," said Dumarest. He had craned so as to see above. "It widens out up above."

Another gallery, this time long and low and bearing traces of mineral deposits. A place to sit and lift the masks and cautiously sniff the stale and acrid air.

Stripping off his mask Axilia rested his ear against the stone.

"Nothing." He shook his head at Dumarest's question. "If the cutters were close we should be able to hear something."

"If they're working. The engine could have broken down again."

"A hell of a time to do it." The miner inhaled deeply, inflating his lungs. "Well, we can stay here for a while. We've air and water and can do without food though we might even be able to find that given luck. Insects," he explained. "Amphibians. Things with no eyes and damp hides. Small usually but find enough and you can get a meal. You'd be surprised what you can find in rocks like this."

"Lichens. Fungi. Molluscs."

"Fish too if there's water," agreed Axilia. "You've had experience, Earl. I guess you'd get along where an ordinary man would starve. A betting man too, right? What odds would you give on us getting out of here?"

"We're alive," said Dumarest. "And better off than we were."

"Alive thanks to you—it's not something I'll forget." Axilia dug casually at the rock with the point of his pick. "Sometimes I think we must all be crazy. Here we are, on a world which gives us all we could ever want, and we turn our back on it. Instead we dig into the ground to get what? Metal which will buy us all we could ever want—or so we think. Me, I know better." He picked a fragment from the crushed rock. Another, a third. "Earl!"

"What is it?"

"Your lamp, man. Shine it this way!" Axilia sucked in his breath as the beam filled his palm with rich blueness. "Well, look at that!"

"Juscar?"

"Lying around for the picking. Look at it!" He grabbed

the lantern and shone it on the roof, the walls. Dust showered as he swung the pick against the surface, blue fragments thick in the debris. "Juscar, Earl, the place is solid with it. Man, we've found the nexus!"

Chapter FOURTEEN

———◦◉◦———

They had dug their way into its very heart and Dumarest sat, thinking, remembering the drawings he had studied, the maps. Had Rudi found the place where they now waited? If so there had to be a way to the shaft in which he had been buried. Finding it would lead him close to the vicinity of the body, the precious medallion it wore.

"Earl?" Axilia turned from where he sat with his ear against the rock. "You moving?"

"Just want to look around. Hear anything?"

"I'm not sure. I—" The miner broke off, lifting a hand. "Something. What do you make of it?"

It was a whisper, a grinding susurration heard through muffling layers of varying densities. The sound of a giant gnashing its teeth. It continued, faded, became loud then faded again.

"The cutter," said Dumarest, straightening from the wall. "Rescue."

If it came in time. If the engine didn't break beyond repair. If the bore had been aimed correctly and could be directed to the narrow gallery or close enough for them to reach. If its vibration didn't trigger a crushing fall.

Things he didn't mention as he left the miner and moved down the gallery. The luck which had kept them alive could change at any moment but, if it did, there was nothing either could do about it. For now it was best to keep himself busy.

The body—where was the body?

The shaft had faced toward the west, turning shortly

155

after leaving the entrance, hitting a gradient and swinging to the south. The tunnel he had used had lain toward the east and the bore he'd reached had been somewhere between. Afterward they had dug themselves up toward the north and east—but at what level?

How to determine the exact point he occupied in this three-dimensional maze?

There was no way aside from shrewd guesswork and instinct. If Rudi had found the nexus he must have come close to the gallery in which Dumarest stood and from it to where he was now buried must lie a negotiable path. But had he found the gallery or had he only hit rich color toward the perimeter?

"Earl?" Axilia's voice rumbled down the gallery. "It's getting louder."

"Good. Keep listening."

Something to keep the man occupied. Dumarest moved to the end of the gallery, shining the beam of his lantern up and around. The walls closed in but there was a crack which could pass an agile man. He stripped off the tanks and padding, the belt and equipment and, retaining only the lantern, thrust himself into the opening. It turned and he followed, rasping a boot against the walls, forcing himself up and around a boss, into a branching junction, a blocked end. Twisting he returned and took the other passage, sucking in his stomach in order to wriggle through, grunting with relief as he emerged into a fissure wide enough for him to stand.

Twenty feet down something glittered.

It was the broken remnants of a bottle and Dumarest knelt to examine it. The neck had been wide, fitted with a screw lid, the container small enough to slip into a pocket. Around the broken fragments glittered others, not of glass. Rising he studied the rock, noting the place where it had been chipped, the mark ringed with minute sparkles.

Past it the fissure turned, widened, rose to turn again and become a shaft, the walls bearing the marks of tools. A shaft blocked by a mass of debris which sloped from roof to floor.

"Earl!" Axilia's voice, by a trick of acoustics, was strangely loud. "Earl, where are you?"

In the place he'd wanted to be, facing where Rudi must be buried, the open air distant only by the mass of debris blocking tunnel and gully. A mass too big for him to move, too loose to be tunneled.

"Earl?"

"Coming!"

The return was a nightmare of twisting and squeezing but the way could be widened. Axilia stared as Dumarest slid through the crack, dropping head first to land on his hands, to roll before rising.

"Man, you look a mess! What did you find?"

"A way out, maybe. The bore?"

"Over to the east. They hit lucky from the sound of it—the cutter broke through into an opening. From the noise it must be near."

Near enough to shake dust from the roof and to fill the air with the music of deliverance. Close enough for them to drive an opening toward it. Five hours later they were safe.

The dinner had been an occasion and one Mtouba had enjoyed. Business was always that but, if it could be combined with social graces, then it gained an added dimension. Now, lifting his glass, he said, "My congratulations, Madam Boulaye. You have worked hard and deserve success. I offer a toast to your continued good fortune."

A toast in which Dumarest joined as did Zalman, the only other occupants of the table.

"Now it's my turn." Isobel refilled the glasses with her own hands. The wine was of the best, provided by the Hausi at her expense, and the food had been to match. "To those who've made all this possible!"

She had been drinking but was far from intoxicated, the sparkle in her eyes and flush on her cheeks created from a more basic emotion than the transitory euphoria of alcohol. Watching her Mtouba knew the toast was a cover for something more limited. She had drunk, not to her associates but to one man alone. One, he guessed, she hoped to keep at her side.

"Earl." Her hand touched his as he turned to face her. "How long will it take to clear the mine?"

"You'd better ask Sven that. He's the expert."

"Without you he'd be dead."

"And without you and the others so would I." Dumarest looked at his wine, seeing drifting sparkles, but they were born of released gases and not from subtle additions. "To work a mine needs a team and no one man is more important than another. Each relies on his fellows. If that trust is absent then work would be impossible."

"Is that why you went after Sven? Because you knew he trusted you?" She sensed his displeasure at the question and quickly changed the subject. "Do you think Sven has the right idea?"

"As I told you, he's the expert." Dumarest set down his glass. "That's why he opened the bore and drove a shaft to the heart of the nexus and beyond. That's why he's working there now."

With Tocsaw and Ocher who hobbled but could tend a hoist and the two others who had remained and who would now collect their reward. Days of hard work resulting in a heap of soft, blue metal with much more to come. The visual evidence of gain and eliminated debt and fat commissions to come. Mtouba had reason to be pleased.

He said, "I've managed to find what you asked for, Earl. A case of freeze-gas; old but it should still be effective. I've taken the liberty of bringing it with me. It's in my raft it you are still interested."

"Earl?" Isobel was puzzled. "What is it you wanted?

"Something to freeze the debris in the shaft where Rudi is buried. Mtouba has found some." Once he'd been sure he'd get paid for it but Dumarest could appreciate the man's caution.

"Why?" She was quick to protest. "Why do we need it? Sven hasn't even mentioned the necessity and, as you said, he's the expert. There's no point in digging out the shaft. We know it doesn't contain juscar. It's effort and expense wasted."

"My effort," said Dumarest. "And my expense. I'll take it, Mtouba. In the raft, you say?"

"Yes."

"Will you drop it off at the mine? Go with him, Hans, tell Sven to have it placed in the blocked shaft." After they had gone he said, quietly, "Why?"

"Why what, Earl?"

"Why don't you want me to find Rudi's body?"

"Did I say that?" Wine splashed as she poured herself more, ruby droplets staining the cloth with the hue of blood. "I just don't want you taking any more risks, my darling. Surely you can understand why?" If he didn't the answer was in her smile, her eyes, the febrile heat of her body as she rose to stand close to him. "Earl?"

"You know why I must find the body."

"To get what Rudi wore around his neck. That stupid medallion." Not the medallion but the information it carried—a fact she chose to ignore. "We don't need it, Earl. With the juscar from the mine we are rich. Rich, my darling, can't you understand? We can take passage to a decent world and buy a house and hire servants and take our place in society. On Ascelius we'd be honored and respected. I have friends there and everything would be so easy. Will be so easy, my darling, if only you'd let me handle things. Forget the medallion. What can it give you I can't? Love? You have more than any other woman could give. Comfort? Luxury? Power? Earl, with me you can have them all. And, if you insist, we can hire men to search for this world of yours. This Earth."

"Rudi believed in it."

"He was a fool!" She saw his expression and looked at her glass then, as if performing an act of defiance, emptied it at a gulp. "Does that surprise you, Earl? Shock you a little? The loving, dedicated wife to speak so of her husband? But to be in love does not mean you must be blind. Rudi had his faults and I recognized them and tolerated them. What harm did it do for him to dream of mythical worlds? All men are boys at heart and it was an innocent illusion. But, for God's sake, don't share in his folly."

"Be reasonable," said Dumarest dryly. "See things my way."

"What?" She stared at him, frowning. "Oh, you're joking, but is it such a joke? I almost died when you went after Sven and became trapped with him. Not all the juscar ever found could have compensated me for your loss. I love you, Earl. Love you—can't you understand what that means to me? You are my life!"

A strong woman and one who would want her own way regardless of others. One who did not hesitate to use any weapon to hand even if it was the weapon of her own body.

As she swayed even closer to him Dumarest said, "We start tomorrow, Isobel. It would help if you were with us."

The place had changed. Lights now dispelled the gloom and the narrow, twisting path had been widened to allow easy progress. Power tools had ripped at the rock in hungry quest of the blue metal, flexible hoses sucking the detritus up and away. Work now halted as Dumarest studied the sloping face of the blockage.

"We need a system," said Axilia. "Have you used freeze-gas before?"

"Not personally."

"Then you might think it easy—most do. Just stick in a nozzle, turn a valve and the job's done. Think that way and you could wind up dead."

"Or crippled," said Zalman. "Hands lost, feet, eyes, faces. You don't have to scare us, Sven. We know enough to be careful." He glanced to where Tocsaw stood with the other two men, at Isobel shapeless in heavy clothing. "All of us. What's to be done first?"

For answer the miner dug a pick into the slope and tugged, scowling at the rain of loose particles. Again he attacked the rubble at different places finally standing to rub at his scarred face.

"Any idea as to just where, Earl?"

"No."

"Then we'll have to take a chance. Adhesion will be stronger at the walls which isn't to say much but every little helps. I guess we'd better hit it here and here and there. Agree?"

"You're the boss."

"Until I hit trouble and then you come to dig me out, eh?" Axilia grunted and shook his head. "In a situation like this instinct can be as valuable as knowledge. Well, what can we lose?" He waved at Tocsaw and the others. "Get busy with those nozzles!"

They were long, thin, perforated with countless holes rammed deep into the slope under Axilia's direction. The tanks Mtouba had supplied contained a blend of chemicals which, when mixed, generated a high-pressure, low-temperature gas of extreme permeability. Blasted from the nozzles it should create a bond to hold the loose detritus by the creation of ice.

"Ready?" Axilia stooped over the couplings. "Here we go!"

Frost whitened the union and nozzles, more coating the slope with a thin, glistening film. The miner lifted a warning hand as Tocsaw moved in.

"Hold it!"

"Why? Let's get at it."

"Sure—and maybe run into a blow-back from an open pocket. If you want to die there are less painful methods. I'll tell you when to start." Axilia lowered his hand, lips moving as he counted seconds. "Right. In you go!"

It was like chopping at a giant sponge made of grit and ice, the brittle matter falling in enlarged granules, in clumps and streams to leave a gaping hole. Quickly the miner curved the upper surface to make a rounded arch, testing as he worked, calling a halt as he pumped more freezing gas into mass.

"Get some shoring," he ordered as the hole widened and deepened. "Move, damn you! Earl, just where the hell is this stiff?"

Somewhere in a space a dozen feet wide and who knew how long? An area bounded by the walls, the floor and the open air at one end, where they stood the other. To clear it all was impossible.

"Isobel?"

She was reluctant, coming forward to stand at the mouth of the opening, face pale, breath a pluming vapor in the numbing chill.

"I don't know, Earl. I was the other side, looking into the shaft, seeing Rudi where he stood. How can I be sure?"

Dumarest was patient. "Try, Isobel. There might be something—you mentioned a lantern." He saw the shake of her head. "Rudi then?" he suggested. "You saw him?"

"Lying, buried, broken—oh, Earl, must I?"

"Lying where? In the center of the shaft? To one side?" His voice grew harsh with impatience. "Which, woman? Left? Right? In the middle?"

"The middle. It must have been the middle."

A slender guide but better than none and the hole deepened but without success. How to tell if the shaft itself ran straight?

Axilia warned as Dumarest ordered traverse cuts, "Be careful, Earl. This stuff's as weak as dampened dust."

"I know."

"I guess you do. Cut too much away and you'll create a trap. One sneeze and the lot will cave in."

A chance to be added to the rest and another to be ignored. The narrow passages delved deeper, formed a winding complex, a low-roofed maze. Crouched, the short-handled shovels rasping at the frozen grit, his hands numbed by the cold, Dumarest squinted through the cloud of vapor formed by his breath at something lying before him.

"Earl?" Zalman whispered the name as he came to kneel beside him. "What's wrong?"

"Nothing."

"Then—" Zalman sucked in his breath as Dumarest plied the shovel. "By God you've found it!"

A thing, old, desiccated, fleshless. A crumpled mass of bone and clothing, the skull grinning in eternal mockery and, between the empty sockets of the eyes, a neat, round hole.

Chapter FIFTEEN

Isobel said, "So you found it, Earl. I wish to God you hadn't."

She had come up behind them, silent on thick-soled shoes, now standing to one side, the gun in her hand as steady as the shovel in Dumarest's own.

"Drop it!" The gun moved a little to emphasize the command. "Just drop it, Earl. You're fast, I know, but, believe me, I can shoot before you could throw it. I know how to use this."

"The university?"

"I was the champion of the pistol team three years running." She nodded her satisfaction as the shovel fell to the floor. "That's better. Now back away a little. More. You too, Hans." The gun twitched toward him, returned immediately to cover Dumarest again. "Back, damn you! Back!"

She was like a spring wound and ready to explode at the slightest touch. Backing Dumarest studied her, the gun in her hand. It was small, a solid-shot thrower, primitive when compared to a laser but just as lethal and far more rugged in field conditions. An ideal weapon for a woman thrust into a hostile environment.

Halting he said, "Why?"

"Why?" Her voice was brittle with tension. "You're always asking that. Why do you think?"

"You were bored, frustrated, angry at the man who had promised so much and delivered so little. But why kill him? Was that necessary? Why not simply leave Rudi?"

"And done what? Gone back home to be laughed at as a failure? The young fool who had trusted an old man and had been taught a lesson?" She felt the pressure of metal against her flesh, the gun hard in her closing grip. God, the wasted years! "Why did you do it, Earl? I pleaded with you to forget him. Begged you to take what I offered but, no, that wasn't enough. You had to chase your foolish dream."

And still had to chase it. The corpse was still buried but the skull and upper part of the torso had been cleared and, around the bone of the neck, he could see a metallic glint. The chain which held the medallion? A few seconds and it could be safe in his hand.

"Earl—no!" Zalman rasped the warning, his face tormented, guessing at the urge, the motivation which would force Dumarest to act against all judgment. "She'll fire if you go for it."

The truth as Dumarest could read for himself. One emphasized with a savage jerk of the gun.

"Back, Earl. Move back!" She watched as he inched farther from the body. "Why are men such fools? You risk your life for an illusion yet scorn the comfort of reality. Wasn't I enough for you? Me and the wealth I own. You could have had it all, Earl. My body, my riches, the house, the mine—everything. Why did you have to yearn for a corpse?"

Her voice was shrill, the glare of her eyes too fixed, too glazed. An animal, frightened of possible attack, trapped and confused would look like that. As would a person driven to the brink of insanity by the torment of guilt and terror.

Dumarest said, gently, "You have nothing to be afraid of, Isobel. No one will judge you. No one condemn. Rudi is dead—let him lie. Just let me get the medallion and we can all leave this place."

"No!"

"Why not? It's cold here. You must be cold. Let's go to where it's nice and warm. Anyway, you promised—"

"Nothing! I promised nothing, damn you! I gave and

you took! I offered and you refused! You refused! You refused me! Me!"

A woman imagining herself to have been scorned and so dangerous. Dumarest eased his legs, the cramped muscles of calves and thighs. The cold numbed and would rob him of speed but more than speed was needed to save him now. Even if he managed to deflect her aim and so avoid the bullet the report of the weapon would bring down the roof. As would her scream.

Zalman?

Reading his question the man whispered, "Don't cross her, Earl. She's a bomb poised to detonate. A word, a look and she'll use that gun."

A man dazed by the obvious, numbed by the death he read in the woman's face, the poise of her body. Weakened by the talent which was his strength.

"Isobel." Dumarest was calm. "Just get the medallion and let's go."

"The medallion?" Frowning she looked at the skull, the chain. Her eyes when she looked again at Dumarest were bleak. "Once you have it you'll leave me. That's all you want, isn't it? All you've ever wanted. That damned medallion!"

"The medallion and you."

"A lie!"

"No. I can prove it."

"How? By using my wealth to finance your dream? That's what Rudi wanted. He expected me to understand him and be grateful. To live like an animal while he amused himself. The patronizing bastard! All I ever had from him were promises. Once we found the juscar we'd go and search for Earth and then we'd be rich and famous—God, how childish it was! How it sickened me! But I needed the juscar. To go back home without it would be to admit failure. Can you understand that? I would have failed!"

To her a shame beyond bearing.

"The fault would have been Rudi's not yours," said Dumarest. "Surely they would have understood that?"

Keep her talking, her attention distracted while he

fought to gain flexibility in legs and back. If he could lunge forward, knock her out before she could fire or scream he had a chance.

She ignored the question. "You knew," she accused. "When you saw the body you weren't surprised."

"No."

"So you knew I'd killed him."

"And I can guess why." Dumarest kept talking, holding her attention, hoping Zalman would move forward toward the precious medallion. A message the man seemed unable to read. "He betrayed you. You relied on him and he let you down. He was weak." As Zalman was weak—why didn't he grasp the opportunity? Inches could make all the difference when the time came to make their move.

"Weak," she said. "Old and weak."

"At first you didn't suspect," said Dumarest. "When you learned the truth it was too much. All your hopes and dreams lost because he lacked your strength of purpose. He couldn't resist the lure of manna. But it doesn't matter now, Isobel. It doesn't matter."

She hadn't heard him. "He laughed," she said dully. "He thought it amusing. He just stood there in the shaft laughing at me and offering that filth in a jar."

"Which you took and threw down the tunnel?"

"I saw it break. Rudi didn't even turn. He just handed me that nugget and told me to go and buy him some more. Ordered me to buy it. The shit!"

"So you shot him?"

She looked at the gun in her hand. "I didn't even know I'd done it. There was a bang and he was down and there was blood and, suddenly, I was afraid. So horribly afraid. But it was all a dream really and then you came and you wanted to find him and it didn't matter because I knew you never could and yet you did and . . . and. . . ."

She was bewildered and Dumarest moved slowly toward her as Zalman grunted and rasped a foot on the floor. A harsh sound which broke the spell even as Dumarest tried to cover the mistake.

"The medallion," he said. "Please, Isobel, the medallion."

"What?"

"Around his neck. You can see the chain."

"Yes." She moved a little, the moment lost, the gun moving to freeze Zalman in his tracks, moving again to halt Dumarest. "That damned chain." She sneered at the grinning skull. "Look at him! My wonderful, intelligent, sophisticated husband. The man who was going to give me paradise on a plate. Daddy!" She kicked viciously at the skull. "Stop staring at me, you bastard!"

The skull rolled, metal glinting from where it rested, a broad disc on which Dumarest could see incised markings. Details lost as the skull rolled back to its former position.

"You bastard! I told you to stop staring at me!"

"No!" yelled Zalman. "Earl—"

Dumarest lunged forward, the roar of the gun a thunder blasting his ears. He saw bullets smashing the fragile bone into flying shards, the slugs pounding at the medallion beneath, tearing into the soft metal, hammering the marks into indecipherable ruin.

A scene lost as the thunder of the gun was echoed by the cascade of dirt from the roof, slamming on the woman's head, pressing her flat as it rained over her body to rush toward Dumarest like water from a ruptured dam. A fall which caught Zalman to smash his chest and stain his lips with the vomit of his blood. Which caught Dumarest's legs and held them for a long, agonizing moment before something wrapped around his waist and almost cut him in half as he was dragged from the detritus which filled his eyes and nose and lungs with vicious chill.

"It was close," said Axilia. "Damned close." His eyes grew bleak with the memory of it. "You were in there too long and I guessed something was wrong. As it was we managed to pump more freeze-gas into the mass as she talked and it held long enough to get you clear."

A matter of seconds but it had been enough. Bruised, frozen by the sub-zero temperature, the line the miner had snaked around his body leaving ugly welts, but, once again, he'd been lucky.

Dumarest said, "You saved my life."

"As you did mine—forget it." Axilia scowled. "A pity about Hans. I liked him." The scowl deepened. "She was mad. Crazy!"

"A woman lost." Anna Sefton set down a pot of steaming tisane and joined them at the table. Isobel's table as it was her house, her supplies. Things she had yielded with the ending of her life but her ghost still remained. "I didn't know her well but I feel sorry for her. A woman trapped, wanting to run yet having nowhere to go. Friendless. Alone."

"A murderess."

"Who paid every second of her life for that one act of impulsive violence. You should understand her, Sven. I know Earl does."

A woman reared in a culture where violence was confined to words and spiteful essays and physical combat regarded as unspeakably primitive. Yet she had tried to break free, had carried her gun with her, had used it when the pressures grew too great. Used it and paid for it with anguish hard for others to understand.

Rising, Dumarest said, "The *Mercador* is due later today. I'll be leaving with it."

"Leaving?" Axilia glared his disbelief. "You can't! Damn it, man, you just can't go off like that. We've things to settle. The mine. The juscar—no, Earl, you have to stay."

To look at a mound, the dirt covering the woman, the ruined medallion, the end of a hope. This world held too many ghosts.

"I'll take what juscar is left after expenses as my share," said Dumarest. "You can have what's left in the mine."

"All of it?" Axilia was dubious. "It's a hell of a lot, Earl."

"You begrudge it?"

"The juscar? Hell, no, you've earned far more than that. I'm talking about what's left."

"You'll have to dig for it," reminded Dumarest. "And settle with the others."

He left to end further argument, mounting the stairs to stand on the roof and look toward the loom of the distant hills. High above them patches of color swirled in smears of orange and green and brilliant yellow; pennants draping the altar of some pagan god, flags fluttering in brave defiance—what had Isobel called them?

"Devils," mused Anna. She had followed and now stood just behind him. She had taken the time to don perfume and its scent was heavy in his nostrils. "Dancing devils—I wonder how often she saw Rudi's face?"

Too often even when blurred by the illusion she had created to explain his end. The lie which had made life bearable and which she had believed so strongly that even Zalman had been fooled. A mistake which had cost the reader of lies his life. Had death been smiling at the jest when it came?

Dumarest said, "Do you blame her?"

"For having killed? No. Who am I to judge? And who can tell when they, too, might do the one deed they will always regret."

The delay, the carelessness, his own impatience—things which had cost him the medallion. A word to Axilia would have kept her from the diggings. His own suspicions should have ensured her absence from the face, but how could he have guessed the extent of her illusion? The savage reaction following the sight of the skull? The madness triggered by the naked bone?

The pain of the lost opportunity was a knife twisting in his guts. The coordinates of Earth, inches from his hand, now gone forever.

And she spoke to him of regret!

As if sensing his mood she stepped closer and he could feel the radiated heat of her body, the stronger scent of her perfume. Feminine weapons used to divert his train of thought from the dead to the living. Yet when she spoke it was of the dead.

"I miss Hans," she said. "He was a gentle and lonely man. One who needed a friend. As Isobel needed a friend and something more. As every woman does. Did you love her?" Then, as he made no answer, she added, softly,

"You must have done. Even if only for a little while. The time it took for you to share her passion—but during that time you loved her. As you must love all women who— Earl, must you leave so soon? Can't you wait until the next ship at least?"

Far above the hills new color rose to join the old; a plume of scarlet caught and shaped by the wind into the form of a somber figure, cowled, faceless. An image which threw blood against the sky.

"I'm intruding," she whispered as the silence lengthened. "You want to be alone. To mourn a little, perhaps. But there is so little time and such limited joy. Sven is a good man but—"

"He's a good man."

Dumarest heard the sharp inhalation as she stepped away. "A good man," she agreed. "And I can make him happy. But, Earl—can you ever be that?"

In the confines of his office Master Elge, Cyber Prime, watched as a galaxy died. First the rim, the thin and lonely stars with lonelier worlds, the blackness eating into the spiral, dulling the sheets and curtains of luminescence, the clusters, the scintillating points, the ebon patches of accumulated dust, the sullen furnaces of red giants, the nacreous fury of white dwarfs, the vivid blues and golds and lambent oranges, the entire spectrum of color which illuminated the firmament. Part by part all died until only a solitary speck hung suspended in the air before his eyes.

Elysius.

A fleck reflected in the orbs shadowed by the arching brows. One which shimmered to move to blink and appear again. The answer to the problem which had threatened his newly won position. The source of the word culled from Nequal's sacrifice.

At his desk Elge touched a button, speaking as a lamp glowed into life. "Continued summation of details appertaining to the Elysius affair. It is now obvious that the attempt to extract useful information from the catatonic unit was futile from the beginning and we still have no clue as to the initial cause of the mental decay. The threat to Central Intelligence therefore still exists. The catatonic unit has been totally destroyed."

As had the other, and Elge paused, stilling the tape, his eyes brooding as he looked at the tiny fleck which hung in the darkness. Had he been premature? Nequal's mind, contaminated by association with the decaying intelligence, had been a danger yet need it have been destroyed? The Council had insisted and he had yielded to the Council—a weakness which never again would he repeat now that his position was secure.

Had Nequal died without cause?

The answer was on record; the man had been doomed before making his offer and yet, even so, he had not totally failed. Again Elge felt the awe of being faced with a mental achievement of stunning magnitude. The doomed and dying mind exerting its full potential to make a final prediction and pass it on in a single word.

Elysius.

Not a world but a position in time and space. One reached by the process of logical deduction, extrapolation, the assessment of all relevant data and the sifting of all probabilities.

To the recorder he said, "Confusion was created by the initial failure to recognize the true meaning of the communication received from Nequal. It was thought the word had been won from the catatonic mind and was a clue to the source of affliction. Now it is certain the word was originated in Nequal's intelligence and comprised the answer both to the affected unit and the threat facing Central Intelligence. The key lies in the secret of the affinity twin which was stolen from the Cyclan and passed to Dumarest. The probability of his having fired on Harge was so high as to preclude any further search for his whereabouts. This, we now know, was an error of gross magnitude. The cyber sent to Elysius has learned that Dumarest is still alive."

As Nequal, deep in his subconscious, must have suspected—why else had his intelligence worried at the problem? Locked in his vat, detached from all physical distractions, he had determined the whereabouts of the one man who could give the Cyclan the domination of the universe.

Elge rose, the depicted galaxy springing to glowing life, touches of color illuminating the planes and contours of his face. Each cyber could become a ruler. The massed brains themselves be given physical extensions so as to seal quickly the culmination of the Great Plan. And he would be the instrument of success. He would capture Dumarest.

One man, moving from world to world as if he were a particle driven by unpredictable forces in a wildly random pattern, but Elge knew better. For each action there had to be a reason and such actions could be predetermined and manipulated once the basic data had been gathered. Dumarest had moved on from Elysius. Had the cyber arrived a week earlier Dumarest would have been taken but there was no point in regret. He was alive and had been found and that was enough.

Elge looked down at his hand, seeing the clenched fist, the fingers curved as if grasping the quarry. Nequal had failed. He would not.

Recommended for Star Warriors!

The Commodore Grimes Novels of A. Bertram Chandler

- [ ] **THE BIG BLACK MARK** (#UW1355—$1.50)
- [ ] **THE WAY BACK** (#UW1352—$1.50)
- [ ] **TO KEEP THE SHIP** (#UE1385—$1.75)
- [ ] **THE FAR TRAVELER** (#UW1444—$1.50)
- [ ] **THE BROKEN CYCLE** (#UE1496—$1.75)

The Dumarest of Terra Novels of E. C. Tubb

- [ ] **PRISON OF NIGHT** (#UW1364—$1.50)
- [ ] **INCIDENT ON ATH** (#UW1389—$1.50)
- [ ] **THE QUILLIAN SECTOR** (#UW1426—$1.50)
- [ ] **WEB OF SAND** (#UE1479—$1.75)
- [ ] **IDUNA'S UNIVERSE** (#UE1500—$1.75)

The Daedalus Novels of Brian M. Stableford

- [ ] **THE FLORIANS** (#UY1255—$1.25)
- [ ] **CRITICAL THRESHOLD** (#UY1282—$1.25)
- [ ] **WILDEBLOOD'S EMPIRE** (#UW1331—$1.50)
- [ ] **THE CITY OF THE SUN** (#UW1377—$1.50)
- [ ] **BALANCE OF POWER** (#UE1437—$1.75)
- [ ] **THE PARADOX OF THE SETS** (#UE1493—$1.75)

If you wish to order these titles,

please use the coupon in

the back of this book.

Outstanding science fiction and fantasy

- [ ] DIADEM FROM THE STARS by Jo Clayton. (#UE1520—$1.75)
- [ ] MAEVE by Jo Clayton. (#UE1469—$1.75)
- [ ] THE SECOND WAR OF THE WORLDS by George H. Smith.
      (#UE1512—$1.75)
- [ ] THE GARMENTS OF CAEAN by Barrington J. Bayley.
      (#UJ1519—$1.95)
- [ ] THE DOUGLAS CONVOLUTION by Edward Llewellyn.
      (#UE1495—$1.75)
- [ ] THE BRIGHT COMPANION by Edward Llewellyn.
      (#UE1511—$1.75)
- [ ] MORLOCK NIGHT by K. W. Jeter. (#UE1468—$1.75)
- [ ] THE GOLDEN GRYPHON FEATHER by Richard Purtill.
      (#UE1506—$1.75)
- [ ] LAMARCHOS by Jo Clayton. (#UW1354—$1.50)
- [ ] IRSUD by Jo Clayton. (#UE1403—$1.75)
- [ ] THE END OF THE DREAM by Philip Wylie.
      (#UW1319—$1.50)
- [ ] WAR-GAMERS' WORLD by Hugh Walker. (#UW1416—$1.50)
- [ ] THE PANORAMA EGG by A. E. Silas. (#UE1395—$1.75)
- [ ] STAR WINDS by Barrington J. Bayley. (#UE1384—$1.75)
- [ ] THE JOAN-OF-ARC REPLAY by Pierre Barbet.
      (#UW1374—$1.50)
- [ ] A TOUCH OF STRANGE by Theodore Sturgeon.
      (#UJ1373—$1.95)
- [ ] MONDAY BEGINS ON SATURDAY by A.&B. Strugatski.
      (#UE1336—$1.75)
- [ ] THE REALMS OF TARTARUS by Brian M. Stableford.
      (#UJ1309—$1.95)

To order these titles,

see coupon on the

last page of this book.

Presenting JOHN NORMAN in DAW editions . . .